EASIER TO KILL

Also by Valerie Wilson Wesley

Where Evil Sleeps

When Death Comes Stealing

Devil's Gonna Get Him

No Hiding Place

EASIER TO KILL

Valerie Wilson Wesley

G. P. Putnam's Sons   New York

Lyrics from *Movin' on Up*, by Jeff Barry and Janet Dubois
© 1975 EMI Belfast Music
All rights reserved. Used by permission.
WARNER BROS. PUBLICATIONS INC., Miami, FL 33014

Excerpt from "Wisdom and War" from *Collected Poems*
by Langston Hughes.
Copyright © 1994 by the Estate of Langston Hughes.
Reprinted by permission of Alfred A. Knopf, Inc.

G. P. Putnam's Sons
Publishers Since 1838
a member of
Penguin Putnam Inc.
375 Hudson Street
New York, NY 10014

Library of Congress Cataloging-in-Publication Data

Wesley, Valerie Wilson.
Easier to kill / by Valerie Wilson Wesley.
p.   cm.
ISBN 0-399-14445-5 (acid-free paper)
1. Afro-Americans—New Jersey—
Newark—Fiction.   I. Title.
PS3573.E8148E18   1998   98-21239 CIP
813'.54—dc21

Printed in the United States of America

1   3   5   7   9   10   8   6   4   2

This book is printed on acid-free paper. ♾

Book design by Ellen Cipriano

For my daughter Nandi,
who always brings me flowers

A belated thanks to Duncan Walton, Ph.D., and Robert Fleming, and my continued thanks to the usual crew, including Charlotte Wiggers, Mary Jackson Scroggins, and Rosemarie Robotham. I also thank Ed McCampbell, M.D., for his medical expertise; my agent, Faith, and editor, Stacy, for their editorial direction; and as always, my husband, Richard, for his love.

To think
Is much against
The will.

Better—
And easier—
To kill.

—LANGSTON HUGHES

CHAPTER ONE

IT WAS THE MOST ELEGANT OFFICE I'D EVER SEEN, BUT THE flowers on the desk made me think about death. They were the same white lilies that had hovered on the edge of every funeral I'd ever been to, and their sweet, sickening smell seemed to hit me no matter where I turned my head. I pushed them out of my mind and tried to focus on the woman dressed in the red Chanel suit sitting across from me.

Her name was Mandy Magic, at least that was what she called herself these days, and she'd clawed her way out of the projects where we both grew up to become the best known radio personality in Essex County. She had a pretty face the color of Kenyan coffee, hair as black and straight as a wig, and a ruby on her finger that was too big *not* to be real. When she'd called last Friday and requested a Monday morning meeting about a "delicate matter," I couldn't believe my good luck. I still didn't believe it.

"I know you're supposed to be a top-notch private eye, but that's not why I am hiring you," she said in the seductive just-this-side-of-phony voice that had pulled radio confessions from hundreds of people and made her a very rich woman. "We have common roots, the Hayes Homes, so I know I can trust you with what I have to say."

"I'm just glad to be of service. Thank you so much for considering me," I said in the fawning just-this-side-of-phony voice that I pull out for people who can pay my fee. I didn't know how common our roots were, but I had no doubt that Mandy Magic could pay the bill. Since most of my clients are as broke as I am, that was enough for me.

"The Magic Hours," her midnight radio show, was the most popular talk/confession show in three states. Everybody listened to it—from Wyvetta Green, the owner of Jan's Beauty Biscuit, who sang her praises daily, to my best friend, Annie, who routinely denied ever tuning in. Mandy Magic's "magical" blend of gossip, weird confessions, and common sense had made her the most admired woman in the city. Her good deeds put many a sanctimonious preacher to shame. High school and community groups regularly counted on her for inspiring keynote speeches and generous donations. She had personally paid the nursing bills for a severely brain-damaged infant, financed the college education of an orphaned teenage boy, and recently adopted a troubled homeless girl. Needless to say, women's groups showered her with tributes, and newspapers sang her praises. She was, as folks were fond of saying, a credit to her race and then some. Yet there were those doubtful cynics who suspected that she was too damned good to be true. I'm ashamed to admit I was one of them.

But my doubts didn't keep me from slipping into my taking-care-of-business gray suit, popping into the Biscuit for an early morning manicure (bestowed, in honor of the occasion, by Wyvetta Green herself), and appearing in Mandy Magic's office bowing and scraping, eager for a liberal helping of her hard-earned bucks. Truth be told, I was a bit in awe of the sister and was flattered that she was prepared to throw her "delicate matter," whatever it was, in my direction.

"I guess you're wondering what I have on my mind," she said, demurely sipping the coffee that we had been served in fragile Limoges cups.

"Whenever you feel ready to share it," I said like some two-bit therapist, as I savored the coffee's caffeine jolt and tried not to spill it down the front of my suit. She put down her cup and handed me a crumpled sheet of yellow paper, holding it by its edge like she might catch something from it. I took it and quickly spread it open. Three words—MOVIN' ON UP—were printed in red block letters across the center. I glanced up, as puzzled as she obviously was. "You're hiring me to find out who wrote you a note?" I tried hard not to sound incredulous.

"And other things."

"What other things?" She shrugged uncomfortably without answering me, her eyes shifting away from mine. "What do these words mean to you?" I asked after a moment, deciding not to push it.

"Just the obvious."

"The obvious being?"

"You know, from that 1970s TV show you can still catch in reruns. What was it called, *The Jeffersons*? It's funny how things like that, theme songs from shows, from commercials even, will stay with you like a prayer."

"What were the lyrics?"

" 'Movin' on up. Movin' on up. To the big time. To that deluxe apartment in the sky. Movin' on up . . .' something like that." She shook her head in frustration.

I remembered and added the words for her. " 'We finally got a piece of the pie'?"

"Yeah. A piece of the pie." She said it as if it embarrassed her, which made me wonder just how much her slice had cost her.

And if you were talking hard, cold cash, this suite of offices had obviously cost her a chunk. There were two other offices besides the one we were in, a modest reception area, and what looked like a small gym in a far corner. This office was, as she emphasized when I came in, her "personal" rather than professional space, which I assumed could be found in one of the radio stations she owned. I couldn't identify the dark, rich wood of the furniture, but every stick matched, and that was more than I could say for the secondhand junk I own. I'd be lying if I didn't admit to a twinge of serious envy when I walked in.

When Newark had been a center of finance and commerce in the early part of the century, this address had been the place to be. But that aura, like everything else after the 1967 riots, had faded even though things were beginning to look up, and thanks to its proximity to NJPAC, the newly built performing-arts center, the building was enjoying renewed popularity. But even during its hardest days, there had been a grandness about it—in the stylishly high ceilings, polished parquet floors, and leaded windows big enough to let in a lot of sun, which put a golden glint on everything this morning, from the red brocade on the seats of the chairs to the ruby in Mandy Magic's ring. She studied that ring for a moment, turning it around on her finger as if she had something heavy on her mind.

"So when did the note come?"

"Last week."

"Is this the first strange letter you've gotten in the mail? You have a lot of listeners, surely some of them are—" She cut me off.

"I didn't get it through the mail. It was left at the front door of this office. But there have been small acts of vandalism, too. Obscene graffiti cut into my door. The tires of my car slashed when it's parked on the street. Small, annoying things that grate on my nerves."

"It could be somebody you know." I chose my words carefully.

She gave me a worried look and rushed her answer, as if she were convincing herself. "Many people have access to this building."

4

"From the tone of the note, the person who left it is probably resentful of your success," I continued, stating the obvious.

"I really doubt that," she snapped and took a sip of her coffee.

"Then what do you think it means?"

"Why do you think I hired you?" she said with a bitchy twist, and I took a sip of *my* coffee.

"Why not call the police, Ms. Magic? Don't you think this may be a matter for them, especially if you really think there is some kind of a—"

"Threat?" she interrupted me. "And please call me Mandy. I didn't call the cops because I don't want my business in the street. You never know where it will go from there, who will overhear you talking to them. There is no threat. The vandalism could be unrelated—it could have been a kid. It's really just the note, that's all."

"Just the note?" I tossed her words back at her, not quite mocking her but saying I knew she wasn't saying all there was to say. She thrust out her chin with a toughness that told me she didn't give a damn what I thought and that she was still the kid who had fought her way out of the ghetto. But she finally gave me the whole story. Or some of it, anyway.

"My stylist was stabbed to death in Lotus Park about a week ago. His name was Tyrone Mason. They said he was the victim of one of several robberies that have turned violent recently, but this note came the day after he was killed."

"So you don't think his death was random?" She didn't answer me.

"Actually, he was more than just my stylist. He was my cousin's son. A second cousin, I guess I'd have to call him. Actually, he was closer to my daughter. My adopted daughter, Taniqua. Much closer. He had only been working for me for about six months." The lack of expression on her face, as she explained his death and her connection to him, told me more about the state of their relationship than her words did.

5

"And this note came—"

"The day after he died. I told you that."

"So you think this note means that he was murdered by someone who has something against you and that he or she is moving on up, from your second cousin to you?" I put it bluntly, and the way she cringed told me I was right. I picked the note up and examined it for some clue that I knew probably wasn't there. "It could still mean nothing," I said, placing the thing back on the edge of her desk yet handling it too carefully for it to mean nothing. "It could just be some cruel prank from somebody who knew about the death of your cousin and wanted to get your attention or scare you for some reason. It could even be from someone who feels you owe him or her something. A message, maybe, from somebody who knew you back when."

"There is nobody left who knew me back when," she said with dead certainty.

"Do you think it could be from someone close to you? Somebody you trust and rely on? And could you be afraid that a person who would write a vague, nasty note like that right after your cousin's death is probably capable of other kinds of betrayals?" I was pushing it, and I knew it, but the way she wouldn't look at me told me that fear was part of it, too. Then her eyes shifted to mine with a sadness that hadn't been there before.

"You ever get the feeling that something horrible is right around the corner waiting to get you, some big old nasty something that will turn your life into dirt and make you wish you'd never been born?"

Her sudden vulnerability touched me, and I smiled both because I wanted to reassure her and because I knew what she was talking about. "A kind of free-floating anxiety? Yeah, sometimes I feel that way, too."

Her eyes left mine again. "That's what that note is to me, Tamara. It's like whatever it is, whoever it came from, is waiting for me, and I've got to know who and what it is before it takes my life."

I was sure she was exaggerating, but I nodded as if I took her seriously.

"I'd like to take this with me," I said, picking up the note again.

Without saying anything, she reached into her desk and handed me an envelope to put it in. I handled it carefully, even though I was sure there were no fingerprints or anything else that would warrant special precaution. "I'd also like to talk to the people on your staff if I could, assistants, secretaries, driver—"

"All I have is family," she said with surprising bitterness.

There was an abrupt knock, and three people filed in as if they'd been listening at the door or were silently beckoned. A thin woman dressed in a dull brown suit led the group. She was followed by a younger light-skinned man, who could have passed for white or Latino, and finally a startlingly pretty young woman, who brought up the rear. The man pulled over three chairs from corners in the large room, and they all sat down.

"I told you what I thought about this idea, Starmanda. There is too much to risk here. Too much could get out. We can get to the bottom of this by ourselves. We don't need some woman nobody knows poking her nose around in your business." The thin woman spat out the words, and her eyes bored into me. But I hardly heard her. I was struck by the name she'd just said.

Starmanda. It was an old-fashioned name I hadn't heard since I was a kid, and it had belonged to my grandmother's sister who had died as a child. But she had lived for me through my grandmother's stories— through the games they played and the toys they made—paper dolls cut from newspapers, jacks made from nutshells, rhymes and hand-claps and foot-stomps that brought back her childhood and made mine richer. I could glimpse Starmanda's presence when my grandmother laughed, and I'd grown up loving that name as much as my grandmother did. Star-man-dah. A mother's way of hanging her daughter's spirit on a star.

1

So Mandy Magic and I had common roots after all. They were in that name and the star somebody had dreamed for her once, too. She may have tacked that Magic business on to make some money, but she had kept enough of "Starmanda" to bind her to her past, and I liked her better for it.

"You've decided then," the thin woman said, bringing me back to her presence and that she was clearly one person who knew about that past.

"Obviously I have."

"You're asking for trouble, Starmanda. I'm telling you that. Digging up shit, spreading it around."

"Asking for trouble, Pauline? I already have it."

"You're making too much of this whole damn thing. It's a goddamn note, for Christ's sake," said the man in a voice with a bored, rough edge to it that made him sound older than he probably was. He looked to be in his early thirties and had a placid, pretty-boy face that was too soft to be fine. He was shorter than I like men to be, but built like a wrestler, his biceps straining against the seams of his brown-and-gray Harris Tweed sport coat. A gold watch—a Movado, I figured—peeked delicately from his sleeve. His fingernails were buffed and neatly manicured.

"Mind your own goddamn business, Kenton." Pauline's eyes were hard, and her voice was high and sharp. He gave a loud, rude snort, showing her what he thought of her.

"This is my own goddamn business, Pauline, don't you get that yet?" His face looked familiar when he walked in, but it wasn't until she said his name that I realized who he was. Kenton Daniels III was the only son of Dr. Kenton Daniels, Jr., a revered Newark doctor and a member of a wealthy family who had founded and supported one of the first free clinics for pregnant teenagers in the city. Although the son had inherited his father's name and money, the good doctor's soul had clearly gone the way of his corpse. Kenton Daniels was a spoiled and lazy spendthrift who traded on his family's reputation and had gone through nearly all of their small fortune in less than ten years. But his gray eyes, what they used to call "good" hair and "old Negro money" contacts kept him in nice clothes and in the presence of women foolish enough to pay for his company.

"Will you all talk to her, tell her everything you can about everything she asks? About Tyrone?" Mandy asked, her voice a pleading whine. Pauline sucked her teeth. Kenton leaned back in his chair, his disapproval written in the smirk on his face.

"Will she find out what happened to him?" The last member of the party spoke, and everyone shifted uncomfortably in their seats. I turned toward the woman, curious about the reaction her words had evoked. I could see the child who peeked through the tight black jersey dress and flash of cheap gold jewelry. Her face was perfectly oval, and the hair that fell in ringlets to her chin was the kind that some folks buy. Her full lips were outlined in a jarring dark maroon lip liner and her large eyes were ringed in black. Except for the gaudy makeup and her haunted, wounded look, she could have passed for a young Lena Horne or Dorothy Dandridge. I assumed she was Taniqua, the homeless teenage girl Mandy Magic had adopted. But whatever age she was trying to be, she was much younger than she tried to look. She threw Kenton a sly sideways glance. He dropped his eyes with a grimace that looked like shame.

"I'll do the best I can," I answered in a matter-of-fact take-charge voice that I hoped was convincing. "I'd like to start right away. I'll have to talk to you further, Ms. Magic—Mandy—as soon as I can." I glanced at her for approval, but she had stiffened like an animal does when it senses danger, her eyes questioning mine as if they were searching for an answer in my soul. "Will tomorrow afternoon be too soon? I'll call you to confirm?" My question stayed unanswered so long I wasn't sure she'd heard it. She nodded finally and stood up, handing me a sealed envelope that I assumed contained my retainer, then she shook my hand to seal our agreement. Her fingers were cold and trembling.

"Thank you," she said.

"Hey, don't thank me yet. You don't know *what* I'm going to find out," I spoke casually, too lightly, and regretted the remark the moment I'd said it. *What in God's name had made me say something so dumb and indiscreet?* Embarrassed, I mumbled an overly formal good-bye, grabbed my bag, and headed for the door. But something made me turn around for one last look before I left them. They hovered around her like vultures after a kill.

CHAPTER TWO

THERE ARE THOSE PEOPLE WHO WOULDN'T FEEL SORRY FOR a woman like Mandy Magic. They might say that with all her money and power she was better off than most of us, so why pity her? They might even say that all she was paying were the wages of fame, so let her weep all the way to the bank. But I knew better than that. Family is all you've got, and if she was calling that crew who sat around her this morning "family," then she was in worse shape than a whole lot of folks I knew. I'd seen both dependency and resentment on their faces, and that combination can turn mean quick. *Crabs in a barrel.* That was what my grandma used to call that ugly edge in folks that makes them begrudge somebody her hard-earned success. *Crabs in a barrel.* Somebody hated Mandy Magic enough to throw a scare into her because they liked seeing her scared. And she was afraid, I was sure about that. Fear

had shadowed her self-confident voice and shown itself in the trembling of her hand. That note could have been from somebody just being
nasty, but there was also that chance it was a warning of something ugly
that was headed her way.

I had resisted ripping open the envelope Mandy Magic had given
me until I got to the garage, and then greed got the better of me. As I
waited for the attendant to bring my car, I tore off the top and grabbed
the check out of its folds with a savage yank. It was a healthy retainer that
could last me a while if I was careful, and the best part was that there
was more to come. When this thing was over, I might even end up
making enough money to add some much-needed dollars to my son
Jamal's college fund, which I wake up nights in a cold sweat worrying
about. As I jammed the check into my wallet, I heard the rumble of my
diesel Jetta as the attendant drove it to the waiting area.

I always have a moment of embarrassment when I claim my car,
a vehicle my son has dubbed the Blue Demon. More often than not,
there is an amused "You actually have the nerve to get into this piece of
junk" smirk on the attendant's face as he holds the door open for me.
He rarely waits for a tip, guessing correctly that anyone who would drive
a car like mine has no bucks to spare. But the guy who held the car door
for me this morning was older than usual. I'd noticed a fifties-style dip
in his walk when he'd gone into the garage to bring the car out. His
tinted aviator glasses were too large for his thin face, and there was no
trace of the wiseass grin I'm used to seeing. His voice was hoarse when
he spoke, like he'd spent the night with a fifth of gin and a pack of un-
filtered Camels.

"I ain't seen no diesels like this for a while," he said as he handed
me my keys. "It go back, don't it? You keep it up pretty good, though.
How many miles you got?"

"Close to two hundred thousand."

He gave a slow, easy whistle through his teeth. "Damn. She's a
good ole girl, ain't she?" I cringed at his words. It kills me when men

refer to ships or cars as "she" like it's some kind of compliment. Considering the Demon's afflictions and quirks, if I had to choose a gender
it wouldn't be female.

"Didn't mean to insult you none, lady. Maybe they do make more
diesels than I know about. I been out of circulation for a while. I didn't
mean no insult to you saying it was old." The man had obviously picked
up but misinterpreted my discomfort.

"No, you're absolutely right," I answered him quickly, feeling sorry
for him; he clearly meant no harm. "The car is old. It was old when I
bought it. It's old now. It's almost as old as my teenage son."

The tension gone, we both chuckled. "You have a boy?" his face
perked up for a moment, and I could see the light come into his eyes,
even behind those glasses.

"Yeah. I do."

"Kids are nice. Do your soul a lot of good. I had myself a little
daughter once, too. A real teeny one, long time ago. Every bit of light
that shined in my life came and went with her." He held his fingers
slightly apart, his muscular, clumsy hands suddenly graceful as they in-
dicated how small his child had been. His eyes, suddenly haunted,
closed for a moment, and I knew that something terrible had happened
to his child and that he had been through some very hard times because
of it. He was a sad person; I could tell that just by looking at him, the
kind of worn-down old man that work, women, and everything but the
blues always seem to leave.

"Thank you, Johns," I said, just able to make out the name scrib-
bled on his uniform. He flinched slightly, and I wished I hadn't called
him by his last name like that; he looked old enough to be my father.

"Hey, Johns, get over here. Got a car for you. The man wants that
red Lexus detailed before he leaves tonight," the white man behind the
cashier's desk called, and Johns's face darkened with resentment.

"I got it, man. I don't usually drive them up. Usually they got me
on wash and wax. Detailing," he said in a whisper, nodding toward the

car parked nearby. I noticed the MM on the license plate and knew who it belonged to.

"That car is something else. Does that MM stand for Mandy Magic?" I leaned toward him confidentially, fishing for any bit of crumb I could get.

"That's what they tell me." He leaned against my car and lit a cigarette.

"What's she like?" You never know when some stray throwaway crack from somebody who has nothing to do with anything will shed some light.

"I ain't never seen the lady if that's whose car it is. Some man, light-skinned dude, always drops it off and picks it up." He nodded upward as if toward heaven.

"Well, what's *he* like?" I was still hoping. He threw me a guarded look, as if wondering what I was up to and if it would be a violation of trust to tell me any more. Then he tossed the cigarette on the ground and polished his glasses on his sleeve.

"Don't know too much about him, either."

"Hey, bro. You better get steppin'," said the man behind the counter.

Johns turned and spat twice in the man's direction, his eyes narrowed in a hatred so naked it startled me. His thick fingers had tightened around the frame of his eyeglasses with enough force to make me think they would snap.

"Take it easy, brother," I said softly. He turned back to face me, a relaxed smile on his lips, as if he were used to coping with anger.

"I'm okay," he said. "Shit can just get to you sometime."

I gave him a five-dollar tip before he left. Mandy Magic's check had put me in a generous mood, and I felt like spreading the wealth around—at least for as long as it lasted. Money brings money, my brother Johnny used to say. I could sure use some money, and by the looks of him, so could Johns.

I'd missed breakfast, so food was on my mind as I drove out of the parking lot. Still feeling the boost from Mandy Magic's generosity, I decided to treat myself to lunch in a spot off Market Street that had once been a church. It was early for lunch, but the buffet table was set up, so I ordered a glass of iced tea and helped myself to a plate of baked chicken, greens, and buttered cornbread, ignoring for once the calorie, fat, and salt content. I settled down at a table close enough to the door to see who was coming in.

All in all, I had to admit it had been a pretty good morning. Mandy Magic's business could end up giving me the professional boost I needed. Although I am thankful for anybody I can get, I know I am the last stop for many of my clients. They usually end up coming to me because the legal system has done them wrong, and they don't have enough money to go anywhere else. Occasionally, though, I do get a different kind of client, one who wants a special service or something done on the sly. They can afford the luxury of secrecy, and they pay their bills quickly and discretely. More often than not, I never hear from them again. But sometimes they recommend me to their friends, which was what I hoped Mandy Magic would do. As I munched my chicken, I allowed myself to savor the fantasy of what a new client base—rich, undemanding, bills paid on time—could do for the quality of my life. If things worked out, I could end up one of those wealthy private investigators who don't have to spend every waking hour chasing down dollars from deadbeats—knowing even as I chased just how tough meeting those bills can be. Hand to mouth. Mouth to hand. That had become my life.

But things could change. Maybe Tyrone Mason's death had nothing to do with the contents of that note. Maybe someone had sent it, gotten their jollies, and would stop with that. I might easily track down the guilty party—somebody harmless and stupid enough to be scared into confessing without too much trouble or risk. Maybe my fortunes would change with this case. Maybe I'd get enough future referrals—

generously offered by a pleased and grateful Mandy Magic—to actually begin to have some kind of savings account, to be able to tuck away enough extra money to consider getting a new car. It was time I junked that damned Jetta, held together as it is by wire hangers, good luck, and prayers. I might actually make enough to lease something decent— a late-model Honda Accord, a Toyota Camry—or buy some furniture that hadn't belonged to somebody else. Maybe I could even put some money down on a computer that didn't take fifteen minutes to boot it-self up. I allowed myself to dream for a moment or two, fantasizing like a kid does about the possibility of a bountiful Christmas. Maybe this was the beginning of a turn in my fortunes.

But on the other hand—and there is always the other hand—there was something disturbing about the whole damn business. Trouble could end up touching her—and me—in ways that neither of us could imagine. She could be "digging up shit, spreading it around," like that Pauline woman told her she was doing. The person who wrote that note had to be somebody close enough to her to know her business and get to her easily. That could only be someone she trusted and would probably rather not know had betrayed her, even though she'd hinted that she feared that it was. With my luck, Mandy Magic would be so dis-gusted with whatever "truth" I dug up, I'd end up chasing her down the street waving my bills in her face like I did everybody else. I took a bite of my chicken leg, finding small comfort in food.

It was half past noon by now, and the office crowd from downtown was coming in for lunch. The afternoon sun beaming in from the stained glass in the cathedral ceiling spread a celestial light on everybody who entered. I settled back to watch them: the women in their smart business ensembles, the men in well-buffed shoes and tailored suits. Important-looking people, well dressed, well fed, sure of where their next paychecks were coming from. People driving BMWs, Mercedes-Benzes, and red Lexuses with their initials on the license plates. I took another sip of tea, wondering for the hundredth time why on earth I had chosen this profession and if it was too late for me to become something else. And then I saw Jake Richards.

I like to watch him walk into a room. Every move he makes is marked by the elegance that some black men seem to come by naturally, an athlete's grace softened with a peacock's-strutting style. He has a drop-dead magnetism that takes over any space he enters and an unwitting charm that enchants juries and women alike and sparks from him like static electricity. If he set half a mind to it, he could be the kind of guy who with a glance can seduce anybody he puts his eyes on. But he is not one of those men. He has too much integrity. He is what my grandmother would call, with a twinkle in her eyes and an approving nod of her head, a *good* man, serious about his work, his people, his family, and those he cares enough about to look out for whenever they need him.

I think I fell in love with him the first time he strolled onto the makeshift basketball court my brother, Johnny, had in our backyard when we were both kids. There has always been a quiet power about him—the way he talks, the way he moves, and in his eyes, which catch you and won't let you go. I watched him make his way toward my table, through the curious, quick glances of women who had filled up the tables around us. The smile on his lips widened as he came closer to me. So did the one on mine.

"Tamara! Hey, it's good to see you. If I'd known you come here for lunch, I'd be here more often," he said in a not-quite-flirtatious voice (but close enough to set a woman dreaming). But his eyes were sad and serious, and for a moment they wouldn't meet mine. "I've got something I've been wanting to run by you if you got some time. So what are you doing here?"

"Case," I said simply.

"That sounds pretty mysterious," he eased down beside me,

squeezing his athletic body into the fragile chair. He was dressed well, lawyer-style, in one of his protect-the-rights-of-the-accused pinstripe suits. I'd never seen him when he didn't look good.

"Nothing wrong with a little mystery in a woman's life." We both chuckled for no reason except it felt good to laugh together. "So what's up with you?"

"What's up? Tam, you sound like one of the kids. Whassup? Whassup?" He hunched his shoulders slightly, lowered his voice to a gangsta-style mumble, and then shot me another of his smiles. But he avoided my eyes again. "Whassup wid me? Don't even ask."

"Come on, Jake. I'll tell you about this case. It's interesting. You'll want to hear it. Big-time celeb," I bartered with him.

"Where is your professional discretion?"

I shrugged my shoulders playfully. "It's all I have to bargain with."

"I know you're not going to abandon your principles for me."

I smiled at that because I've certainly considered it once or twice. Jake is married, sadly, sometimes forlornly but definitely. I've known his wife nearly as long as he has—both before and after the mental illness that has changed both their lives. But he loves her. I am as sure of that as he is now, although there have been times in my life when I wish it were otherwise. But then he wouldn't be Jake, and my feelings wouldn't run as deeply as they do.

Yet there has always been an unspoken, occasionally scary, attraction between us. My grandmother used to tell me that to call a feeling by its name will give it life. "If you call it by its name, you have to reckon with it," she'd warn us in her often illogical but loving attempt to protect us from some evil thing she feared would harm us. "Don't call it by its name." So Jake and I never did; both of us danced around the spark of our attraction, never reckoning with any of the feelings we had. But there is always a price paid for ignoring the truth; the piper will eventually demand his due.

"My principles? What principles?" I answered him finally, and we both laughed, both of us knowing that was anything but the truth. "You can help me with one thing, though. What do you know about Lotus Park?"

"Not a nice place. Unless you're a gay man who doesn't like being gay and who likes dangerous, secretive sex. Don't go there at night."

"Hmm. That kind of place, huh?"

"Yeah."

"There was a killing about a week ago. They said it was a robbery. Did you hear anything about it?"

Jake thought for a moment. "Well, I do know there have been some very violent robberies there recently. Mostly suburban white guys looking for some black or brown action who end up getting more than they can handle. A couple of muggings have turned very ugly—face slashings, beatings, that kind of thing. As a matter of fact, I do remember hearing something about a stabbing last week." He glanced over the top of his glass at me, a touch of amusement in his eyes as he tried to figure out what I was searching for. "So is this your big-time-celeb case?"

"Maybe," I flirted back. "Do you remember anything else about it?" He thought for a moment.

"They said it was a robbery," he leaned back in his chair for a moment and sighed a wistful sigh. "Funny how things stick in your mind. I used to play in Lotus Park when I was a kid. My daddy used to take me and some of the other kids on the block over there and try to teach us how to play like Jackie Robinson. I didn't know exactly who Jackie Robinson was, but I wanted to play ball with Pop." He drank some of his water, gulping it as if he were swallowing his memories. "Yeah, the park's definitely changed. Maybe that's why I remembered it when the cop mentioned it.

"This was the first killing, I think, though. Mostly it's just been slashings," he continued. "Maybe somebody overheard somebody yelling something about money. I don't know. Maybe it will come back to me."

19

"The guy who was killed was named Tyrone Mason. He was a hairstylist who worked for Mandy Magic. Does that remind you of anything?" He thought again, narrowing his eyes slightly as he concentrated.

"Mandy Magic? That's the radio lady, right? I don't remember his name, but I do remember hearing somebody say something about her. It could have been the same dude. I can't think of any other reason I'd connect her name with Lotus Park." He shook his head and sighed. "The hustlers who operate out of that place are definitely not nice little boys."

"And you're sure it had something do with a robbery?"

"Yeah. That much I do remember."

So maybe Tyrone Mason's murder was just a robbery gone bad, and the note probably was just what it seemed. I took a sip of my tea, strangely relieved as I studied Jake's face for a moment. Something *was* bothering him. I could tell just by looking at him.

"Jake, what's going on?"

"I probably shouldn't even bother you with this, especially here, but you know, you're sitting here. I'm sitting here. Jamal and Denice are *not* sitting here—"

"And it has something to do with Phyllis?" I answered for him, imagining her face as I said her name.

If you saw her on the street, you'd never know she is mentally ill. She is a feather of a woman, with eyes that sometimes shine much too brightly. She speaks in a shy, hesitating manner that makes you want to finish her sentences, and if you didn't know her well, you'd probably miss that strain in her voice when she tries to answer simple questions and that distant, frightened look in her eyes. When I was young, I'd seen her aloofness as mysterious and interesting. People were always drawn to her strange beauty. I'd always envied that elusive quality she had, as if she didn't quite hear you or was thinking of something else. All the men I knew seemed to flock around her, vying to take care of or protect her, and they always had—from her father when he'd been alive, to Johnny in his own awkward way, and finally to Jake. But it wasn't until after her marriage and the birth of Denice, her first and only child, that her illness broke through and those fits of rage and suspicion that come from nowhere took over her life.

I have never been sure of her diagnosis, except that she is under a doctor's care and spends time—sometimes weeks—in a hospital. Her medication, when she takes it, makes her calm but leaves her listless yet easier for the rest of us to deal with. But she told me once that it dulls her feelings and takes the joy out of her life. So sometimes she doesn't take it. She gives herself a break.

I am the only person Jake ever talks to about her. His marriage is filled with secrets, and I know nearly every one. There are times when I wish I didn't know so much, that we didn't have the history we have, that I didn't know so many of the dark corners in his life. But I don't have a choice anymore.

"No, not Phyllis, not directly anyway. It's about Denice," he answered me after a while. His only daughter, Denice, is a couple of years younger than Jamal, not quite a teenager yet but moving toward it. She is a quiet girl who has the fragile beauty of her mother, but her gentle spirit and charm are all Jake. My heart skipped when he said her name, and the anxiety that I'd seen on his face was now on mine.

"What happened?"

He took a sip of his soda, thinking for a moment before he answered. "I can't put my finger on it. She's changing in a way that bothers me. Maybe 'bothers' is too strong a word—'concerns' maybe is better." He was choosing his words like a lawyer, not wanting to say something he didn't mean. But I could see in his eyes that "bothers" was the word he meant.

"Tell me!"

"You know she's always been shy. Reserved, like some sweet little old lady with too much on her mind." I smiled because he'd nailed her shy, proper personality. "She's a typical teenage girl in a lot of ways."

I nodded sympathetically even though, having raised a son, I knew nothing about typical teenage girls. But I had watched the stages of her life go past as I'd watched them with my own child—the preoccupation with body and appearance, the insecurities, the occasional know-it-all arrogance. But I'd never watched too closely. My own kid was enough for me.

"I've seen some things in the last couple of weeks that are beginning to worry me."

"Kids always worry you, Jake."

"No. It's more than that." His eyes bored into mine, warning me not to dismiss this. But I wouldn't have because I'd seen parts of that little old lady that worried me too. The timidity, the distance. A part of her that didn't let anyone in, not even her father, and certainly not me. She was his child, but she was Phyllis's as well, and I had always wondered how much of her mother was inside her, how much might someday break out. A chill went through me as I read, then spoke, his thoughts before he did.

"I don't think an illness like that, the kind that Phyllis has, can be passed on, Jake," I said too quickly. "Whatever it is, Jake, I don't think it's that." I didn't know for sure. Sometimes mental illness did seem to run in families, and I knew that unspoken fear haunted him. I understood that fear well. I had my own "bad blood" to worry about: My mother who liked smacking her kids around. My father who handed what was left of his life to a bottle of bourbon. My brother who put a loaded gun into his mouth and blew himself to kingdom come. Everyone has some "bad blood" in them somewhere.

"It's not that so much," he said, "but maybe it is. I worry about her so much. I wonder sometimes if I've given over to my wife some of what I should have given to my daughter." His eyes clouded with that mix of memory and sadness that comes whenever he talks about Phyllis.

"What is it then?"

"Small things. I wonder how much she has been affected in ways that I haven't even been aware of until now." He sighed hard and shook his head in frustration, then began again. I reached across the table and took his hand, holding it for a moment. "What are some of the things that have happened?"

He thought for a moment. "The way she closes up. Her secretiveness. It's almost as though she is afraid to tell me things that bother her, like she doesn't want to burden me. I wonder how much of her I've sacrificed to do right by Phyllis. This illness has affected her too. I'm beginning to ask myself, how much more should I give up? For Denice. Even for me. I don't like to ask myself that question. Do you think I have that right, Tamara?"

"You have to answer that yourself. I wish I knew the answer, but I don't."

"This isn't a conversation that we should be having here, in the middle of the day, over greasy chicken and iced tea." He chuckled self-consciously as he tried to change the subject, obviously uncomfortable, the way men sometimes are when they share what they feel. "You always bring out what's real in me, Tam."

But before I could answer him or even return his smile, there was the click of stiletto heels, the smell of Diva perfume, and Ramona Covington, moving with a cat's stealthy grace, was at our table.

I have never been one of these mean-spirited women who begrudge other women their hard-earned due. I am proud of my sisters, honor them when I can, and cherish them for the support and kindness we often show each other. But Ramona Covington always brought out the worst in me. I hadn't started off disliking her; it had grown in spurts. I'd first met her about a year ago when she joined the District Attorney's Office. She was a hotshot young prosecutor who had resigned from the state prosecutor's office in Trenton because she'd wanted to be "closer to the action," as she put it.

She is a woman who seems to have everything—strong mind, nice clothes, great car, and even though she is a few years younger than me, I was slightly in awe of her. I've always admired superachieving sisters who stride over mountains without missing a step. I'd even invited her to join Ujamaa House, an organization of take-care-of-business women that I'm proud to belong to. But when I'd told Ramona that our organization was made up of women—all kinds, all jobs, all income levels—her eyes had glazed over and a condescending smile had settled on her lips.

"Black women don't have any power. Why should I join an organization with people who are all less powerful than me?" she'd said with a barely concealed sneer and absolutely no sense of shame. I have to admit, I held it against her.

Today, as usual, she looked great. I'd seen the suit she was wearing in the Short Hills Mall for four hundred bucks, and it looked better on her than it did on the mannequin. She had light-brown eyes, a pretty square-jawed face, and a body that bragged *personal trainer.*

"Thank God, Jake, I caught you," she didn't so much say as purr. "Can you spare a few minutes? Something important has come up with the case we were talking about earlier." From some spiritual reserve within me, I pulled out what passed for a smile and let go of Jake's hand.

"Ramona, you know my friend Tamara Hayle."

"Yes, we've met." She threw me a cursory glance of recognition that said she had about as much time for me as she did for the woman who did her nails and quickly shifted her gaze back to him.

He had told me recently that he admired Ramona's grit and her invulnerability. "You know that there is nothing you could say or do that would ever really hurt her. She plays hardball as tough and mean as any of the guys on the other team want to play. She's got a kind of take-no-prisoners style that you find yourself enjoying," he'd said with that look of wide-eyed admiration men usually reserve for professional athletes.

I was reasonably sure that Ramona's take-no-prisoners style touched every aspect of her life, and she was sharp enough to know a good man when she saw one. I wondered about the kind of hardball she'd play if she knew the only thing standing in her way was a mentally ill wife and a troubled teenage daughter. I was sure about my principles, but I'd bet hers were about as honorable as a horny young jock on steroids.

"Do you have a few minutes to go over it with me?" Ramona said to Jake, tilting her head charmingly to the side like a little girl before she asks her daddy for a dollar.

"Sure," he said more quickly than I felt he should have.

"I think we'd better talk about it back at the office. Some of these things are pretty confidential," she added with a condescending smile in my direction. I stared at my iced tea, not wanting to risk picking it up.

"Okay," he said after thinking for a moment, and rose quickly. "Guess we'd better head back," he said to me. I watched him closely.

Did he really look eager to leave with her or was I imagining it?

"Tamara, I'm sorry to interrupt your lunch. But will you excuse us?" Ramona smiled a shark's smile.

"Sure," I said graciously and shot her back one of my own.

"Call you?" Jake asked and then added much more seriously, confidentially. "We've got to finish talking about this thing. I have another idea, about—about—her that I want to run past you."

"Sure, Jake."

"Friday night?" he said over his shoulder as he left.

"Sure, Jake. Talk to you then," I said cheerfully but not feeling very cheerful at all. *Sure.*

I watched them, involved in earnest conversation, as they weaved their way through the crowd.

Was there an intimacy between them as they occasionally bumped against each other?

I felt vaguely sick for a moment, then made myself stop. Jake and

I were friends; we always had been and probably always would be. He was a grown man with enough good sense to see through any play she might try to make.

If he wanted to see through it.

And that was the point; that was what was bothering me. But maybe that was his business, too. Life didn't turn out the way it did in romance novels. The bad guys won sometimes. And so did the bad girls. But Jake Richards was nobody's fool.

I felt a nagging sense of sadness—jealousy, I finally had to admit, because I'm not a good liar, even to myself. My feelings for Jake, sliding as they do between friendship and something else, were confusing and complex. Maybe I just didn't know him as well as I thought I did. Maybe there were parts of him, having nothing to do with me, Phyllis, or Denice, that he also had to answer to. Parts that were simply off-limits to anyone but himself and whomever he chose to share them with. Maybe that was the truth of it.

I got up after a while and went out to my car, Jake and Ramona Covington still heavy on my mind.

Had there been some intimacy between them, and did I really want to know?

Spotting the Blue Demon sitting in the parking lot amid the BMWs and Baby Benzes didn't improve my mood. With its predictable wheeze and lurch, it kicked itself into gear, and I backed it out of the parking lot, my day darker than it had been two hours ago.

The restaurant was located near my old neighborhood, and like a homing pigeon I headed toward it, trying to push Ramona and my fears about her and Jake out of my mind as I pulled up to the building where I had grown up. The projects. The slums. My home. They were abandoned now and stood like ugly monuments to somebody's dream that you could pile families like egg crates on top of one another and nothing would end up broken. The Hayes Homes. They'd been named for somebody dead probably before my time. Maybe he'd blessed them or lived long enough to curse them out. Nobody probably gave a damn now one way or the other or probably ever did. The windows were boarded up or broken and stared out like long-dead eyes. Shattered glass and shards of steel littered lots where grass had never grown and was probably never meant to. I thought about the families who had lived there once—the Jameses, the Greens, the Thomases—and us, the Hayles, all gone now. Many families had survived and thrived, and they had left, their spirits and wills stronger for the experience. I was stronger for it—I knew that now.

I studied the old buildings, trying to remember where all those families had lived, but they were skeletons, picked clean of flesh and life. The bottom floors had been gutted to be imploded like so many other buildings in the city, like people's dreams had been.

My thoughts went back to Jake and Ramona for a moment and then just to Jake and his love for Denice, now shadowed by his fears about her mother. And that brought thoughts of my own mother, and her face, contorted in anger as it often was, came back to me.

They didn't call it abusive back then. They would just say that she didn't spoil the child by sparing the rod, but her "rod" could be anything from the back of her hand to a brush or a frying pan that she'd just dumped the oil out of. The first curse words I ever heard flew out of that woman's mouth. I wake up nights, wondering if the damage she did us all has eaten up some part of me I never missed because I didn't know I had it.

I brought you into this world. I can take you out!

She would say those words, her eyes ablaze as her rage turned her face into one I didn't know. To this day my heart beats fast when I think of it. I took a deep breath, pulled it in tight, made myself think of something else, something good.

My son.

He gives me all the things my mother thought I took from her. Or maybe it had nothing at all to do with us—with me and Johnny and my sister. I didn't understand it then. I thought I would after I'd had my child, but I didn't. I probably never will.

Yet there had been more to my childhood than my mother. There was my sweet grandmother down the hall with her tales and games and the ribbons she tied in my hair. My brother and sister, as cozy as twins in the small dark room we all shared. My father and the smell of English Leather and cheap bourbon that traveled around him like an aura. All of us tucked away in these buildings that had been our home. I glanced at them now, thinking about another woman who had grown up here like I had.

She had come a long way from this lonely place, empty of everything but memories. Closing my eyes, I tried to recall the hidden anguish of my childhood, and I wondered which of Mandy Magic's secrets these dark walls still kept.

CHAPTER THREE

I FOUND OUT ONE OF THOSE SECRETS THE VERY NEXT AF-
ternoon. I was walking up a deserted street on my way to visit Mandy
Magic when I saw him. His face was partially hidden by a black wide-
brimmed hat worn down over one eye, TV gangster–style. His cheeks
and chin were pockmarked and scarred. The suit he wore was stylish
and fit him well but was made of a red-and-green-checked material that
had a cheap gleam to it. He was comical and sinister at the same time,
always a dangerous combination.

He leaned against the side of a black late-model Lincoln, watching her brick and wood-trimmed Tudor like he wanted to move in.
When I walked past, he cocked his head to one side, as if he had heard
something disturbing. He had street instincts. I knew that because I
have them, too, and mine were tingling. Our eyes met for an instant.

His were piercing, the kind that can peer into a woman's soul and see every bit of weakness. I wondered what he was doing on a street in Belvington Heights on a Tuesday afternoon. He was probably wondering the same thing about me.

If I had to name the one place I like least in Essex County, it would be Belvington Heights. As pretty goes, it's a pretty town: stately old one-family homes that could easily house a couple of generations; lawns the size of public parks; addresses so discreet that at night you need a flashlight to illuminate them, given the stingy glow from the nineteenth-century-style gaslights.

I used to be a cop in Belvington Heights. I'd chosen it over my hometown because it seemed a safer, saner place to cut my teeth as a rookie, and with a kid to raise, I didn't want to risk a bullet from some baby gangsta over bullshit. But some bullets rip your spirit deeper than your flesh, and that was the kind I got hit with in Belvington Heights. In an attempt to "diversify" its all-male, all-white force known statewide for its "enthusiastic" protection of the "rights" of its fine white citizens, I was hired—the lone African-American, lone woman. I quit after three of my brethren in blue picked up my son and beat his babysitter and some of his friends to within an inch of their young lives basically because they were black in Belvington Heights after-hours. They claimed the boys resisted arrest and were disorderly—that old song and dance cops trot out when they're looking for a legal excuse to whip somebody's ass. I know that the distant rage that comes into Jamal's eyes whenever he remembers it will be with him for the rest of his days, and I can never forgive them for that. I don't like driving through the town, even though these days there are more black and brown faces on the streets and in the stores.

But everything about this man told me he was not one of those new faces. I could feel his eyes on my back as I walked past him, gliding up and down my body like invisible hands. I turned around to face him, returning his stare. He climbed into his car in slow motion and drove off. Unnerved, I watched him go and then continued on my way.

The flagstone path leading to the house was narrow, and tall hedges on either side gave some privacy but not as much as they should have. The house itself was small, with leaded windows, wood trim, and an oval red door that belonged in a fairytale. There was some distance between this house and its nearest neighbor, which made it seem vulnerable and exposed.

I glanced around to see if the man had come back but couldn't see much over the hedges. I rang the doorbell and heard the click of approaching high heels. There was a pause, and then the slightly husky voice of the young woman who had been in the office yesterday. She asked me to identify myself, which I did, wondering why she hadn't been able to see me through the peephole in the door.

"It's the way it's made," she explained after she had opened the door with a nod toward it. "If a person stands a certain way, kind of far back and off to the side, you can't see who it is." Her eyes shifted quickly toward the street and then back to me.

"You're Taniqua, aren't you?" I asked, even though I knew who she was. She looked more like a kid today, even though she was dressed all in black. Her pretty face was mostly clear of makeup, but I could see a smudge of mascara as if she'd been crying. She wore a loose-fitting black T-shirt and tight black jeans, and her pretty hair was bunched back and tied with a black ribbon. Her tiny feet were arched miserably high and shoved into a pair of killer pumps. A butter-soft gray leather coat had been carelessly flung onto a chair by the door. I wondered if she had just come in. "I'm Tamara Hayle, a private investigator. We met yesterday," I said.

"I know who you are." She spoke with a teenager's bored matter-of-factness; her eyes glanced behind me again toward the street.

"Are you looking for somebody?"

Her eyes came back to mine. "No. What makes you think that?"

"There was a man out there before, and the way you were looking, I thought you might know who he was. Do you know who that man was, Taniqua?" I spoke in the stern, now-tell-me-the-truth-because-I-can-tell-if-you're-lying tone I use with Jamal, even though I had no reason, save instinct, to think she was lying. But the wide-eyed innocent look she gave back made me wonder.

"No."

"Just curious," I said with a shrug, deciding not to push it.

"I'll get Mandy."

"Mandy?"

"Haven't you noticed? Everybody calls her Mandy." She gave a naughty smile and then shouted, "Ma, somebody here to see you."

"Who is it?" The familiar voice floated down from another part of the house.

"That lady who you saw before. Tamara Hayle."

"Take her into the living room, and tell her I'll be right down."

"She'll be right down. Follow me." Taniqua took out a stick of gum and pushed it whole into her mouth. Sashaying through the foyer, she added a pronounced swish that definitely didn't belong to any teenage girl I'd ever seen. But her exchange with Mandy Magic had been so typically teenager-and-mother it made me smile. She nodded toward a couch covered in pink and green chintz, and I settled down on it and listened to her click her way down the hall and back upstairs.

The room was small but as exquisitely laid out as Mandy Magic's office. It had a cozy elegance to it—a Laura Ashley fantasy of English country living. Dying embers from a fire still sparked in the fireplace even though the day was warm, and a magazine lay open in the seat of the easy chair as if somebody had just gotten up. A large cut-glass bowl of roses, nearly the same shade of pink as the flowers in the chintz, and an intricately carved ebony box sat on a mahogany coffee table. A thin silver cigarette case sat between the box and the flowers. Always nosy, I glanced around the room—making sure there were no hidden cameras anywhere—and after a minute or two cautiously snapped open the gold clasp on the ebony box. Two silver pistols, as neat as pins, lay side by side in red crushed velvet. They looked like antiques, and I touched the carved ivory handle of one of them, tempted to pick it up. I wondered if they were loaded, thought about checking, and decided that with my luck one would probably go off. I closed the box and then, fighting my finger's itchy impulse to open it again, made myself touch one of the roses in the glass vase instead. They were fake, which didn't surprise me. Real flowers with falling petals and fading blossoms would have been as out of place in this room as a pot of chitterlings simmering in the kitchen. Or a loaded gun. I got up to see what I could see of the rest of downstairs.

The house was surprisingly small for the Heights. As far as I could tell, there was only this room, a small dining room across from it, and a kitchen off that. The winding staircase, which was of the same wood parquet as the floors, led upstairs to what were probably two small bedrooms. When I heard Mandy Magic coming downstairs, I scampered back to my perch on the couch, settling my hands demurely in my lap. Like her daughter, Mandy Magic was casual today. Her straight black hair was pulled back off her face, and she wore a red warm-up suit and fluffy red and blue house shoes. She was much smaller and more physically fragile than I remembered from our meeting yesterday. I stood up when she came into the room—humble employee to respected employer.

"Thank you for meeting with me. I just needed a few more facts about things—a few more questions about Tyrone Mason and other things—that you weren't able to give me in the office," I said after making the conventional remarks about the beauty and comfort of the room. I pulled out my black-and-white notebook and asked her for the home telephone numbers and addresses of Pauline Reese and Kenton Daniels III, and she gave them to me without hesitating, although she looked as if she weren't quite comfortable doing it. She reached for a cigarette from the silver cigarette box then put it back in the box and playfully slapped her own hand.

"Very bad habit. Very bad for my voice," she scolded herself.

"But hard to break," I added sympathetically.

"Nothing is hard to break if you're determined to do it. What do you want to know? It just takes discipline and determination." Her eyes locked intensely with mine. She seemed tougher than yesterday, or maybe it was just that she was in her own space, talking on her own terms.

"Well, to start, do you know a guy who drives a big Lincoln, a weird-looking brother, sinister?" I asked her offhandedly, closing my notebook, hoping to surprise her and watching her closely for a reaction.

"Why do you think I would know somebody like that?"

I shrugged. "There was a guy like that parked out in front of your house a few minutes ago. I thought maybe you—"

"Is he still here?" she interrupted, not hiding the hint of alarm in her voice.

"I think he's gone."

"To answer your question, no. Nobody I can think of." The control was back in her voice, but her eyes flitted to that cigarette case before they came back to me. I studied her for a moment, getting ready to use the now-tell-mama-the-truth tactic I'd used earlier on her daughter, but she changed the subject, reminding me, I figured, who was paying the bill.

"You said earlier you wanted to know about Tyrone Mason. Shall we start there? He was the son of my cousin, Harold Mason."

"So your name is actually Starmanda Mason."

"No. My name is Starmanda Jackson, and we won't go into that. But Jackson doesn't work as well as Magic anyway, if you know what I mean. You can't have a magical touch with Jackson." She gave me a quick self-deprecating wink that made me smile. "That is my real name, though, Starmanda Jackson, after my mama, not after my foster parents.

But that's confidential, right?" She said with a strange smile of pride, and I nodded that it was, wondering at the same time if she really thought that her fans or anybody else actually believed that her real last name was Magic. Who did she think she was fooling? Who would care?

"Could you tell me something about Tyrone?"

"Like I told you before, he was closer to my daughter, to Taniqua, than to me. Good hairstylist. His death was violent and unfortunate. That's really all I can say." She cut it short. I glanced at her in surprise.

"That's all?" I wondered if she'd forgotten I was working for her and not the *National Enquirer*. Had she decided to forget the whole thing?

"That's what I said, didn't I? There is not much more to say."

"Before, in your office, I got the impression that you didn't care for him."

She shook her head, indicating that I'd misinterpreted her, and then continued diplomatically. "He was a young gay man who was finding himself. He may have been searching for some answers in that park and found some that cost him his life."

"So now you're accepting the police version of his death?"

"I don't know what to accept."

"So there was no tension between you." She hadn't exactly said that she didn't care for him, but the tilt of her head and tone of her voice had implied it.

"Maybe you misinterpreted me." She opened the silver case and took out that cigarette she had obviously been thinking about. I closed my notebook, leaned back against the couch, and counted to ten before I spoke.

"So you have nothing else to tell me about Tyrone?"

"No, not really. He was my cousin's son, like I told you. He worked for me like I told you. And he was tragically murdered. By we don't know who. Shall we go on?"

"And now you think he was just a random victim of serial robbers who stabbed him to death?" She didn't react, so I continued. "And so now you *don't* believe that mysterious anonymous note and his death are related, and all you really are concerned about is finding out who wrote that note, right?" I didn't bother to take the sarcasm out of my voice.

She glanced at me with surprise and annoyance. "What are you getting at? I never told you I wanted you to look for the person who murdered Tyrone. That is for the police to do. All I want you to find out is who wrote the note."

She was backtracking fast, and I didn't know why. I'd gotten the idea in the office that Tyrone Mason's death *was* the reason she was so worried about that strange note. I searched her face for an answer, but it was inscrutable.

"What if the two things are related?"

"What if they are not," she said in an even voice as if she were convincing herself.

"Has someone said something to frighten you, Ms. Magic . . . Mandy? For some reason you are having second thoughts; your feelings about this whole thing seem to have changed. You seem to be afraid of something."

"Do I look like the kind of woman who scares easily?" I had to admit that she didn't.

I placed my notebook down on the table, wondering as I did it why, considering the size of my bank account, I was about to say what I was going to say. But I was disgusted. "Something has changed." I said what I knew.

"Nothing has changed."

"I'm afraid this is a waste of my good time and your good money."

Despite the fact that most of my clients don't have the proverbial pot for pee, I can always count on them to tell me the truth or what they know of it. Sometimes they have difficulty pulling it out, but they trust me enough to tell it. I can see the pain in their eyes when they finally face it. I couldn't for the life of me figure out this woman's game. Despite her healthy retainer, I didn't like being lied to, and I sensed this woman was lying. I've never been one to take somebody's hard-earned money for no good reason, even if they hand it to me. "Why did you hire me, Ms. Magic?" I added, back to formalities. "I think you're hiding something from me. I don't know what it is or why, but I sense that you are. What do you really want me to find? Or not find? Do you really think that your life is in danger? I honestly don't get it."

"I want you to find out who wrote me that damn note." Frustration and anger were in her voice. I stood up dramatically, picking up my things.

"I think you'd better find somebody else." She stood up too.

"There is nobody else."

"You've got a lot of money, Ms. Magic. I can guarantee you that you'll find a new investigator much more quickly than you think. I even have some names for you. But I can't deal with clients who aren't going to level with me. Things can get too dangerous out here for me and for you too. I have to know the whole story and who all the players are."

She put a hand on my arm, and I shook it off. "I'm sorry. Will you wait? Please."

"I feel as if you're playing two sides of the field. That there are things that you are afraid for me to know. Tell me what is *really* going on here."

"I've told you. I want to find out who wrote that note."

"Why does a note scare you so much?"

"Because I know there will be more."

"How do you know that?"

"Call it instinct. Please work with me."

"Why me?"

"Because I trust you as much as I am able to trust anybody. I don't trust a lot of people. We come from the same place. We grew up in the same way."

"I don't think so, Ms. Magic. Don't kid yourself."

"Please call me Mandy."

"Who is that man?

"Which man?" She looked puzzled.

"The man I asked you about a minute ago. The one who was outside your house when I drove up. The one you said you didn't know," I added after a moment, and I could tell she knew whom I was talking about.

"Him?"

"Yeah, him."

"Somebody who knew me back when. And please let it go at that—don't make me go there now. Not now. He has nothing to do with this."

"Has he threatened you?"

"No."

"Who is he?"

"Was he."

"*Was* he then?"

"He was my pimp," she said the words as if she still didn't believe them, and I sat back down. There was very little change in her face, and I'd looked for it; only her upper lip trembled slightly. She pulled it tight into the lower, like kids do when they won't let themselves cry.

"I'm sorry." I wasn't sure why I was apologizing, whether it was for the past, the present, or how hard I had pushed her for the truth and how far back she had to go to get it. She lit that cigarette she'd been holding with a rueful bite of a laugh.

"Yeah. I'm sorry, too."

I waited for a while before I spoke again, giving her time to catch her breath and myself time to let this new piece of information sink in. "Does this man have a name?'

"Rufus. Rufus Greene."

"Rufus Greene," I repeated the name to myself remembering that Rufus is Latin for red and thought about his tacky red and green suit. Just like a damn pimp. "Could he have sent that note? Or have been responsible for Tyrone's death?" I asked, very cautiously starting from the present instead of the past.

"No." She said it as if she had never been more sure of anything in her life. "He didn't do either thing."

"Why are you so sure?" I asked despite her certainty.

"He has no reason to do it. He risks as much as I do. Don't waste your time or my money chasing down that lead. I think there must be others who—" She stopped herself and glanced away.

"Others who what?"

"Have more to risk."

"How do you know?"

She turned on me, not with shame but defiance. "Don't you think I know that man as well as I have known any man in my life? I know what he will and won't do like I know every wrinkle in his big black dick."

I dropped back against the couch. I had to give the sister that one. But I stuck Rufus Greene at the top of *my* list. "Let's go back to Tyrone Mason, the truth this time." I said it gently, like I was speaking to a child.

She took a drag on her cigarette and then stubbed it out. "He was a low-life bastard," she said quietly.

"He had been working for you for about six months before he was murdered?"

"Yeah. About that."

"Why was he a low-life bastard, Mandy?"

She paused a moment. "He was blackmailing me." I could see pain and embarrassment in the lines that were suddenly visible around her chin and on her forehead. "I trusted that stupid little fool, took him in like I did, and all the time he was just trying to get paid." I wondered as I watched her how many other members of her family were just trying to get paid.

"Was he close to any other member of your . . . family?"

"He was nice to Taniqua. When she came into my life, he seemed to go out of his way to be kind to her. He was the first person she really bonded with. That's why I kept him around."

"So Taniqua came into your life about six months ago?"

"No. I adopted Taniqua three years ago. When she was fifteen."

"But Tyrone was still part of your life even though he wasn't working for you?"

"Indirectly. I saw him from time to time. My cousin died about two years ago. We made contact then." She paused for a moment and then added. "The Masons—that family they placed me with—were very dysfunctional, they would call it today. I got out, ran for my life. Not everybody else did. I loved my cousin, Harold. He wasn't really my cousin, but I called him that. But he had a lot of problems, and he may have passed some of them on to his son, Tyrone. But that may have made him sensitive to Taniqua."

"So Taniqua has a lot of problems, too."

"Yeah."

"And Taniqua's problems are—"

"They are over now."

"So when did Tyrone start blackmailing you?"

"Right after he started working for me. He'd found out that I was a teenage prostitute. He never actually said that I should give him money to keep him quiet, but he implied that somebody else would tell, that he'd heard it 'on the street,' as he put it, and if I didn't pay, it might get out. He offered to act as a middleman. To deal with the person, to keep him quiet. But he couldn't fool me. I knew he was involved."

"And you have no idea who was working with him?"

She sighed, "No."

"Probably the person who is writing those notes?"

"I don't know."

"So how much did you give him?"

"Twenty thousand in all. Ten thousand the first time he asked. Another ten right before he died."

I rocked back in my chair at the mention of that sum." Why didn't you tell me all of this in the first place?"

"I didn't want it to get out. Nobody else knows. Nobody. Not Pauline. Not Kenton. Nobody."

"Well, somebody does. The person who was working with Tyrone."

"Maybe it will stop now. Maybe nothing more will happen."

"I wouldn't count on it."

"People respect me now," she continued, as if she hadn't heard me. "Do you know what it would do to me if people found out that I was a teenage whore? That I've done the kinds of things I've done? That I've even known people like Rufus Greene?"

Probably increase your audience, I thought cynically but didn't say.

"Has anyone asked you for money? Tell me the truth now." I said it with tolerant annoyance, like you might chastise a mischievous child.

She thought for a moment. "No. It was just that note."

"And Rufus Greene, showing up here like he did," I added. "Does Taniqua know Rufus Greene?"

"No." She looked at me straight, but somehow I knew she was lying.

"Did Tyrone have any friends that he was close to? Did you see him hanging out with anybody on a regular basis?"

"No."

"How about Kenton?"

"You'll have to ask him. I don't know. It was mainly Taniqua, though. He meant so much to her for some reason. She even kept his personal effects after he died. I am his last known relative, and when his landlord called, I kept them. I was going to throw them away, but she saw them and asked me for some of his things, so I let her have them.

Wasn't too much. Some cheap gold jewelry that Taniqua wears around her like a charm. A couple of photo albums that belonged to his father. Not much at all. I never told her what he tried to do. I didn't want to go into any of it. I guess you will have to talk to her too, won't you?" Her voice was suddenly worried—and scared.

"If you don't want me to start with Taniqua, then I won't," I said gently. "But if you want me to get to the bottom of this thing, eventually I'll have to talk to her. Tyrone may have said something to her that may be important."

"Maybe you should start with Pauline. She knows where all the bodies are buried."

"And there are more bodies that have been buried?" I said only partly joking.

"There always are," she said with a sad, strange smile. She paused for a moment and then went back to her daughter. "Taniqua's life is like mine used to be. She is pretty like I used to be, fragile. Trouble always seems to find her, always standing around in the shadows, waiting for her. Even though he was a bastard, Tyrone was her friend, and his death affected her more than anything else since she's come here. It has shaken her loose from all the structure I tried to give her, all the protection I tried to build around her." She looked at me as with an almost startled expression in her eyes, as if she had just remembered something important, and her tone was suddenly girlfriend-confidential.

"They always get you in the end, don't they?"

"Who, Mandy?" I asked, wondering if she was talking about Rufus Greene or Tyrone Mason.

"They always snatch you back into whatever hole they crawled out of, drag you right down there beside them like you never left, right down there where they think you belong." I studied her face for a moment without saying anything.

"Do you feel guilty about moving on up? About leaving so much behind you?" *Survivor's guilt.* I didn't say the words, but that was what I meant.

"Sometimes." She sighed then from so deep within her that I knew she was telling the truth. At least for the time being. I heard steps approaching the room, not the clickety-clack of Taniqua's heels, but somebody else. Kenton Daniels III strolled into the room like he owned it.

"I'm taking the car later on if that's okay with you."

"Taniqua said she wanted to go to the mall." Mandy glanced at me and then back at him.

"I'll take her." He settled into the easy chair, picked up the magazine, put it down, and then studied me curiously as he rested his size-nine loafers on the fragile mahogany table.

"I'm Tamara Hayle. I think we met at the office yesterday. I'd like to make an appointment for an interview if I could."

"Yeah. Anytime. That's cool. Got nothing to hide." He picked up the silver case, played with it for a moment or two, and then put it down. Mandy watched him without saying anything.

"Are you by any chance related to Dr. Kenton Daniels?" I asked him.

"Yeah. He was my old man. Why?"

"He was a great man. I had a good friend who was a patient of his once," I gushed, realizing the moment I'd said it what a dumb lie it was.

"A pregnant teenager during the late sixties?" His gray eyes studied me with unconcealed amusement. "You don't look that old."

Before I could think of something to take the egg off my face, Taniqua strolled into the room, and a wide grin broke out on his face. I wondered just how safe Mandy Magic was keeping her.

"Incidentally, Mr. Daniels, I'm not as young as I look. And I'm a lot smarter too." I added awkwardly, adding a cocked eyebrow that I hoped relayed that if he was up to what I thought he was, he might fool Mandy Magic, but he wasn't fooling me, especially when it came to pretty young girls in tight black jeans. I stole a glance at Mandy Magic, who had ignored our exchange, which struck me as odd. How many other things, I wondered, did she choose to ignore? Kenton rose and, without a word to either of us, left the room with Taniqua, his arm draped loosely around her shoulder.

"So how old is Taniqua now?" I asked as soon as they were out of earshot.

"Just turned eighteen," Mandy said. She seemed to be lost in her own thoughts.

"Age of consent?" I said it with a chuckle that could have passed for a joke, but neither of us thought it was funny. Something about the girl told me she had probably been consenting for quite a while.

"I don't even like to think about what I was and what I was doing when I was eighteen." Mandy's voice was strangely wistful. "I was born grown, Tamara. I never even had the luxury of turning eighteen. Taniqua didn't either. She has had it tough too, tougher even than me in her own way."

"Does it trouble you, her spending so much time with Kenton Daniels?" I was taking a leap into dangerous water, and I knew it, but it was a question that had to be asked. She grunted a laugh.

"Taniqua can take care of herself. She always has. A man like Kenton Daniels, I don't worry about him. He may flit around Taniqua all he wants, but he sure won't land."

"So you don't feel like he's taking advantage of you or that he will take advantage of her? Can't he—and both of you—hurt her? Isn't it your responsibility to protect Taniqua from men like that?"

Her eyes were hard when they turned to me, and I wasn't sure if her anger was aimed at me or Kenton Daniels.

"She *is* eighteen. She sure ain't a child no more."

"Why do you put up with it? With him? A man like that?" I continued, still not understanding why she was as indifferent as she seemed to be, and why her voice had suddenly taken on a coarser, meaner edge.

It was almost as if it were someone else talking or as if those words had once been said in that same way to her.

I brought you into this world. I can take you out!

She stared at me for a moment, and then tilted her head as if she'd just thought about something. "You don't know much about men, do you?"

"Excuse me?" *Where had* that *come from?*

"Men." She spit the word out like it burned her mouth. "You don't know much about a man like Kenton Daniels, anyway. What do you think this is about? Fucking? Fucking ain't nothing but fucking—that's all it is. Like animals do. Like somebody can pay you to do. It don't mean shit. Taniqua can learn things from a man like Kenton Daniels that a better man, maybe a more honorable man, could never teach her. I got where I am with the lessons I learned from men like Kenton Daniels. Men who look like devils and end up being angels in disguise," she added in an almost dreamy voice.

"Angels in disguise?" *Had I heard her right?*

"That's what I said."

"So you keep a spoiled lowlife like Kenton Daniels around to teach your daughter painful lessons?" I didn't disguise the contempt in my voice.

"He won't touch her. I can tell you that much."

"How do you know that?"

"I know men. I told you that. And Taniqua learned very early to take care of herself."

"Like you learned it?"

"Like I did."

"Who gave you the pistols?" I asked out of the blue, wanting to throw her off balance, to see something in her eyes besides the cool control that had taken over, and I saw it for an instant: surprise and then alarm.

"I bought them for myself."

"Do you keep them loaded?"

"What good is an unloaded gun?"

"Have they ever been used?"

"To duel with? Come on!"

"You know what I mean."

"Not yet," she said with a crooked grin.

CHAPTER FOUR

I HAD THREE PEOPLE ON MY MIND THE NEXT MORNING AS I walked across the street to the Jan's Beauty Biscuit: Rufus Greene, Tyrone Mason, and Mandy Magic. I was sure Wyvetta Green could help me answer the questions I had about all three, so I'd stopped by Dunkin' Donuts earlier for two dozen doughnuts and a couple of cups of coffee as an offering. I don't like to call the fact-finding conversations I have at the Biscuit interviews, but that's what they are, and Wyvetta is too sharp to allow herself or her customers to be pumped, even discreetly, for information without getting something in return. We never discuss this rate of exchange; it's an unspoken understanding. Often I'll get my nails done and give Lucy, Wyvetta's manicurist, an extra-generous tip. Sometimes I'll get my hair touched up or trimmed when it could easily and obviously go for another month. Some days I'll take Wyvetta out to lunch at the Golden Dragon down the street. Every now and then I'll do some investigative work for her, although she usually pays me what she can for that. My offering can be as generous as treating her and whoever wants to come along to snacks and drinks after work or as cheap as it was this morning. It doesn't much matter to Wyvetta, as long as it's something.

I'd tossed yesterday's conversation with Mandy Magic around in my head most of the night and still wasn't comfortable with my feelings about her. I didn't trust her. I was sure she was still lying, but I wasn't sure about what. Yet I also admired her strength, her survivor's guile. She had turned her life around and become the success that she was; however, it still seemed odd that she could never tell the whole truth about anything unless it was dragged from her. I couldn't figure her out.

I finally decided that I needed to give myself a dose of professional detachment. Far be it from me to judge the woman's style of parenting, which I found disturbing, or feel that it was my responsibility to understand her. I wasn't her shrink. She had hired me, paid me *good* money and obviously needed help that she believed only I could give her. God knows she wouldn't be the first client I had mixed feelings about, and chances were she wouldn't be the last. But we had a deal, and I had to live up to my part of it. And that brought me to the Biscuit with coffee and doughnuts in hand.

Jan's Beauty Biscuit has been around a very long time, and I was sure that Wyvetta knew something about Rufus Greene, who wasn't the type of character you easily forgot. I also knew that I might be able to find out more about Tyrone Mason and his death and if there was still even a remote possibility that it could be more than the cops thought it was. If hairstyling had been a part of his life, at one point or another he'd probably found his way through the doors of Jan's Beauty Biscuit. If so, Wyvetta Green probably knew more about the man than he wanted her to know. Dust mop in hand, Wyvetta was just opening shop when I strolled in laden with pink and orange Dunkin' Donuts boxes and a large leaky bag of coffee.

"Well, Miss Tamara Hayle, what you got here? All this for me? I can sure use a cup of coffee and some of them doughnuts." Wyvetta leaned the mop against a nearby wall and quickly relieved me of the bag and box depositing them on a table in the corner of the shop. I grabbed a doughnut and a cup of coffee and relaxed in one of the leatherette chairs, inhaling the varied smells — Lysol, hair-straightening chemicals, perfume — that always seem to cling in the air. In the last couple of years, Wyvetta and her boyfriend, Earl, have done a fair amount of work on Jan's Beauty Biscuit, which she named after her mother, Jan, and her favorite food. She keeps the place meticulously clean. Everything sparkles, from the stainless-steel sinks to the cerise chairs and pink-and-white-checked tiled floor.

As I did every morning, I checked out the sister's hair, which changes colors, lengths, and styles on a weekly, sometimes daily, basis. I've seen it long and short, and I've seen it blond and red. It's been sprinkled with silver and striped with gold. She's worn it piled up and slicked down. She was fond of saying it was a living advertisement for her product, and that she spared neither time nor money in promoting it. But she was wearing a scarf this morning, which was pulled turban style around the top of her head and tucked in at the nape of her neck. There was also a distinct greenish cast to her pretty brown skin. She noticed what I'd hoped was a discreet stare and screwed up her nose in annoyance.

"Don't say nothing about it. I've been listening to Earl's mouth about it all month long." She gave a chocolate doughnut a hearty chomp as she settled down in the chair next to me.

"Is it makeup?"

"Halloween is right around the corner, Tamara, but even I'm not that far-out. It's a facial mask." She grimaced in the mirror and then arched her neck examining her skin carefully. "I'm supposed to wear it before I go to bed, but Earl's been carrying on so about it at night, I decided I'd wear it for a couple of hours in the mornings and wash it off before my customers start coming. It's almost done its job, anyway. All these enlarged pores I got around my nose are almost gone." She examined her face slowly and critically in the mirror and continued, "It's not like Earl don't have his peculiarities. I been telling him for years about that damned gold tooth he got stuck up in the front of his mouth. Men ain't nothing but spoiled babies when you come down to it." She shook her head wearily.

I nodded sympathetically and took a bite of my whole wheat doughnut. "So what's wrong with your pores?"

"Look," she brought her face close to mine and pointed out invisible spots on her nose and cheeks with her fingertips. "Enlarged! They're almost gone now since I been using this mask, but you can still see some of them if you squint."

"They're a little hard to see," I said diplomatically as I studied her flawless skin.

"Well, that's because this mask is wearing them down. I got to hand it to Petula Lincoln — the girl knows what she's talking about." She got up and went into the back room and came back with a tiny jar of green-colored cream, screwed off the top, and handed it to me to sniff. "Smells good don't it, just like limes." I rubbed a bit between my fingers, smelled it, and gave it back to her.

"Who is Petula Lincoln?"

"My new cosmetologist."

"Cosmetologist?"

"Helps my customers with their cosmetics. Does facials, gives you creams and masks to help with certain skin conditions. She called about a month ago. Told me she goes around to salons doing facials and selling products. Asked if I was interested, and I told her yeah, so she added the Biscuit to her list of regulars. She's been coming through here once a week to sell face creams and body lotions and do facials if somebody wants one."

"She lives around here?"

"Bloomington. But she's spreading out. My customers seem to like her. So it's working out fine. Earl cleared out some space in the back, and that's where her table is set up. She should be coming by today. I'm surprised you haven't seen her."

"What does she look like?"

"Tiny little woman. Short blondish hair. White."

"Her hair is bleached white?" I tried to picture her.

"No. *She's* white."

"With a name like Petula Lincoln?"

"I was surprised when she walked in, but I sure wasn't going to turn her away because of her color. We seen too much of that shit ourselves to go and do it to somebody else."

"Petula?" I said, still considering the name. "Maybe she's English, like Petula Clark, the singer."

"Naw, she ain't English any more than I'm Indian. But she did say her friends call her Pinky."

"Pinky?" I said, thinking about Rufus Greene and wondering why all these folks named after colors were showing up in my life all of a sudden.

"That's what she said so that's what she told me to call her. The customers call her Petula. I did have to tell her, though, that she might have to make a couple of adjustments because of the race thing."

"What kind of adjustments?"

"Well," Wyvetta said after a pause. "Not many black women want to have some 'European process' done to their skin. And I told her she should deep-six that peaches 'n' cream skin powder and come up with some mango 'n' plum or something like that. Most everything she sells is named after some kind of fruit.

"And to tell the truth, I was a little worried about how my customers would take to her. You know we can get to talking about white folks pretty bad up in here sometimes. The Biscuit is a place where people have to feel free enough to say what's on their mind without hurting nobody's feelings. That's part of the place's charm." Wyvetta glanced around her shop with obvious pride, and I nodded in agreement. I'd certainly been the beneficiary of more than my share of useful gossip from her loose-lipped customers.

"So what did she say?"

"Said white folks can get to talking about black folks pretty bad, too, and she always figured it cut both ways so that didn't bother her one way or the other. She fits right in. Folks say what's on their minds, and she even puts in her two cents worth every now and then. Good times and bad men don't know no color, and Petula Lincoln has seen her share of both."

"Speaking of bad men, Wyvetta, ever seen or heard of a guy named Rufus Greene?" I was anxious to get some information before anybody came in.

"Rufus Greene the pimp? Oh, Jesus!" Wyvetta screwed up her face in disgust. "Tamara, why you want to go mentioning that man's name before I get my breakfast down good?"

"So you know him?" I asked eagerly, putting down my cup.

"No! Not on a *personal* basis," she said with a proud lift of her head.

"You've heard of him then?"

"Yeah. I've heard of him." She put her coffee down on the table and added a packet of sugar. "He's probably too old and ugly to pimp anymore, but during the sixties and early seventies he was sure out there spreading around his evil self. In the old days, some of his girls used to come in here to get their hair done. Bastard," she spit the word out. "If there's two things I can't stand in this world it's a pimp and a woman beater."

"And he was both?"

"Well, he was a pimp and that should tell you something right there."

"What did the women who worked for him say about him?"

"Why you want to bring his name up?" Wyvetta said, picking up her coffee and taking a fast sip. "That was so long ago I put anything I might have heard out my mind right after they said it. It don't do to carry stuff about people who ain't no good around in your head. Bad for your spirit."

"If you can think of anything at all, it would be helpful. He's connected to a case I'm working on."

"Why on Earth would you be working on a case involving a man like that?"

"Sometimes you end up working with or for people who, if you'd known from the beginning who they were, you wouldn't have gotten involved," I said, thinking again about Mandy Magic.

"I guess everybody has to make a living," Wyvetta said philosophically, answering her own question.

"Do you think any of your regulars would know about him?"

"If they did, they damn sure wouldn't admit it." She got up and washed her hands in a nearby sink, as if she could wash off Rufus Green with soap and water. She got another doughnut and sat back down. "To tell the truth, I never heard all that much about him. He had a couple of girls who worked for him. Far as I could tell, they did straight up-and-down business, no drugs or kinky-winky stuff or anything like that. He wasn't as bad as some of them, I don't guess. One of the girls used to say he protected them. They turned tricks and gave him money to protect them, and it was nothing too much more than that. He didn't try to string them out or anything. But the man who run him out of town was a straight-up drug peddler, I do know that." She sighed and shook her head sadly. "They were some pretty girls too, the ones who came in here. It was the late sixties, early seventies and there was supposed to be more opportunities for our people then, but those girls had to fall back on that. I could never understand how girls so young—and not one of them was much past eighteen—could get involved with some mess like that. Where were their mamas? But they say don't make fun of nobody's feet until you walked in their socks, so I guess I got to leave it at that."

I smiled at her mangling of the old expression. "I think it's don't criticize somebody until you've walked a mile in their shoes, but I know what you're saying. You don't know what happened to the girls who worked for him or what they did after he left town?"

"I have no idea. Maybe they found somebody else to work for. I haven't heard his name for damn near twenty years. The only reason I remember it was because he had the same last name as me, and I was always scared he'd end up being some distant relation or something. But he spells his name with an *e* at the end, thank the Lord!" she added, lifting her eyes toward the ceiling.

We sat for a moment, silently munching doughnuts and sipping coffee, each lost for a moment in our private thoughts about Rufus Greene and the wages of sin.

"How about Tyrone Mason?" I asked Wyvetta after a while.

"Tyrone Mason! Girl, you hittin 'em out the park today, aren't you? Don't tell me you're looking for something on Tyrone Mason too. What does he have to do with Rufus Greene?'

"Nothing. Two separate cases," I lied.

Wyvetta chuckled. "I was wondering when you were going to get around to asking me about somebody's business I know about."

"Oh, go on, Wyvetta. You know I don't ask you about anybody's business." I widened my eyes in innocence.

"You're talking about the hairdresser, the *stylist*—as he liked to call himself, right?" I grinned when she said it because I could tell by the glint in her eye that she was eager to tell it all, as only Wyvetta could.

"Of course. And where else would I come if I wanted to find out something about a hairdresser but to the best hairstyling salon in Essex County?" Wyvetta was never above having her ego stroked, especially when it came to the Biscuit, so I laid it on thick.

"Five minutes ago you were asking about a pimp and his whores, and I don't know what the hell you think I'd know about that!" She cracked a smile, so I'd know she wasn't insulted. "He was murdered a week or so back in Lotus Park? Lord, I remember seeing something about it in the *Star-Ledger*." She bowed her head slightly as if in silent prayer.

"That was him."

"You know he worked for Mandy Magic, *the* Mandy Magic." Her eyes grew big with admiration, which didn't happen very often. I wondered how big they'd get if she knew everything I did.

"That's what I heard."

"Tyrone Mason," she repeated his name to herself, as if she was thinking about it. "He worked for me a couple of years back. Damn, this stuff pulls your face right tight." She touched the side of her face.

"Maybe that's how it tightens your pores. So, how many years ago?"

"Three." She got up and went to the back room, and I heard her shuffling around boxes and crates. She came back holding a thick maroon photo album with the words "Jan's Beauty Biscuit" printed in gold letters on the cover. She opened it slowly and began to turn the pages, occasionally holding something up for me to see.

"Here's Mama," she said with reverence, as she pointed to a photograph of her mother—Jan Green, who except for her conservatively styled and pressed hair, was a dead ringer for her elder daughter. She gazed at the photograph for a moment, sighed, and then turned to another page. "I always do a group photo about once a year, just to keep a record of who has worked for me and how far I've come—or haven't come. Here I am, and the people who I had working for me in my first shop," she pointed to a group photo of a younger self and two women who looked even younger than she did. The shop looked as if it had just been opened. The walls were pale yellow and none of the chairs matched. "I figure if they worked less than a year then they really wasn't with me, but Tyrone, I think he was here for at least a year." She turned the pages and pointed out another photograph. "Here he is. There's the little girl who used to do manicures before Lucy."

I examined the group photograph of the three, taken before the pink and cerise renovation; the chairs were black and the walls a weird shade of tan. Wyvetta hadn't aged a bit—same size, same smile—but the hair, of course, was different. The woman was obviously younger, and the man was gauntly handsome with a smoothly shaved face except for a neatly trimmed mustache on his upper lip. He was dressed stylishly in what looked like an expensive sweater and nicely cut slacks and had a clean-cut, college-boy look about him, but he wore a curious, artificial smile, as if he were mocking the whole scene.

"Sneaky little bastard," Wyvetta said under her breath. I glanced at her in surprise.

"Why do you say that?"

"Had a lot of the weasel in him." Wyvetta closed the book and took it back into her storeroom, talking to me over her shoulder. "Slipping around, talking about people behind their backs. I have to admit, Tamara, when I heard he kicked the bucket, I didn't cry no tears." When she came back, a disagreeable scowl had settled on her face, as if the mere thought of the man brought back unpleasant memories. I went to the table where she'd put the doughnuts and broke a cinnamon one in two, giving half to her.

"So why did you hire him?"

"Looking for something that wasn't there. I liked the boy at first. He had a kind of boyish, teasing way that appealed to the mother in me. But I knew within two weeks of hiring him that I wouldn't want that sucker for no son of mine."

"He got on your list fast." She took a snapping bite of her dough-nut, as if it were part of Tyrone's anatomy. "So what did he do?"

"Name it, that boy did it. Lie. Steal. Cheat. Nothing big-time, but little things. We was talking before about how folks in the Biscuit get to telling their business and everybody else's? Well, he might hear some-thing from somebody, and next thing you know he'd be trying to use it against them. Real subtle-like, smooth, but definitely doing it. You know I couldn't have nothing like that going on around here."

"Blackmail?" Mandy had told me as much, so I wasn't surprised, but I wondered if he had other victims.

"I guess that's what you could call it."

"And that's why you let him go?"

"One of the many reasons. Now I don't mind if somebody takes a drink now and then or smoke a little weed on their day off, as long as they don't do it in here. Even me and Earl been known to take a nip out that Johnnie Walker Red he keeps stashed in the back at the end of the day. But this place *belongs* to me," she said with a proud nod of her head. "Their day off is their day off, if you know what I mean. I ain't gonna be runnin' no drug tests on somebody or anything like that. But I'll be damned if I want somebody working on one of my customer's heads all tanked up or high. I'll be damned if I'll ever allow that kind of mess in my shop, named after my mother and all." Her face darkened with outrage at the thought of it, and she narrowed her eyes angrily. "He spent a lot of money on things that did him no good," she said quietly, obviously not wanting to talk badly of the dead.

"Do you ever remember seeing him with anyone who struck you as a criminal type?"

She glanced at me critically. "Tamara, what's a criminal type? You know I don't make assumptions about people unless they give me rea-son to."

"Somebody who looks like they could stab a person to death in Lotus Park. You know he was murdered in that park?"

"I can't remember seeing anybody like that with him. Nobody deserves to die like that. Not even Tyrone. Do you know if they found the person who did it?"

"No. I don't think that they did." She looked up at me, the light of sudden insight shining in her eyes.

"You're trying to find out who killed him, aren't you? I knew there was something funky about the way that boy died. And Mandy Magic, you're working for her, aren't you? And she has all that money to make wrongs things right, to find out who killed that boy like that. He must *not* have done her as bad as he done me for her to be caring about him enough to pay somebody to look into his death. He did have some talent with a comb and a can of spray, though, I'll give him that. Girl, that Mandy Magic is something else, ain't she? What a *good* woman she is. A good, solid black woman!" Wyvetta, on a roll and nodding her head from side to side for emphasis, sang Mandy Magic's praises for the next five minutes. I kept my thoughts to myself.

"Hold on, Wyvetta," I said finally. "I haven't mentioned Mandy Magic, so don't be telling anybody—"

"Tamara Hayle, you know I don't tell your business any more than you tell mine." She was obviously hurt by my suggestion.

"Well, I have to be careful."

"So do I. I never repeat anything that has been said within the walls of the Biscuit. It's kind of like church."

"So how long ago did he work for you?"

"About three years ago." I tried to put the times together in my head even though I didn't think it meant much. He was working for Wyvetta around the time that Mandy had adopted Taniqua. But she'd said he had made contact with her around the time his father, her cousin, had died, roughly two years ago. He may have known Mandy Magic during the time he worked for Wyvetta, but he may not have had any contact with her yet.

"Did he ever mention Mandy Magic to you?"

Wyvetta put down her coffee. "Mandy Magic! No. I'd sure remember it if he had. He must not have known her then. If he had, that fool would have found a way to brag to us about it."

But he probably had known her, and considering the kind of man both women said he was, the fact that he didn't find a chance to mention it at the Biscuit said that he gained something important by keeping his mouth shut. If Wyvetta's customers spoke as freely to him as they did to everybody else, then someone may have inadvertently mentioned something about Mandy Magic's past life. Maybe one of Rufus Greene's women had sat down in his chair one day and mentioned a pretty young girl named Starmanda Jackson, and he'd tucked that bit of information away until he could make it pay. Maybe even Rufus Greene himself had crossed his path. He had procured young women once — why not young men?

"Did Tyrone ever visit the Biscuit again after you fired him?" I asked Wyvetta.

"Oh yeah, girl. He made it a point to come back by here, driving a big, fancy car, bright red. Said he had an apartment in some fancy condo in Bloomington. Splendor Heights or something like that. Said it like I was supposed to have heard of it. Newark and East Orange ain't good enough for some of our folks once they think they got something."

"So Splendor Heights is in Bloomington? That's not exactly Hillside Drive in Belvington Heights."

"Well, it's got more white folks than Newark, and some folks put a lot of stock in that." Wyvetta shrugged and shook her head in wonder. "Ask Petula, she might know something about that condo where he lived. Yeah, my man had done pretty good for himself, considering how he left. Somebody was paying the boy good."

There was a hesitant knock on the door, and Wyvetta beckoned in a slight white woman with short blondish hair, which the morning sun gave a pinkish hue. She was shorter than both of us, with a small, elfin face that was older than it looked at first glance. She was probably in her late forties, close to Wyvetta, but the fine lines around her mouth and eyes were more visible even though her heavy makeup was well applied. Another living advertisement for her own product, I assumed. She was dressed all in pink and pulled a small pink-and-white suitcase on wheels behind her, which brought to mind a traveling Barbie. Her polyester beautician's uniform was exactly the same color as her coat. It worked nicely with Wyvetta's decor.

"Petula Lincoln, Tamara Hayle. Tamara Hayle, Petula Lincoln. This is the famous private investigator who works upstairs." I cringed slightly, as Wyvetta waved her hand in my direction.

"I've heard a lot about you," Petula said in a high, girlish voice that could probably get on your nerves if you heard it often enough, but her handshake was warm and sincere. I caught a whiff of bananas as she came close. Another advertisement. "Wyvetta, how come you have it on now?" Petula shifted her attention to Wyvetta's face.

"Earl," Wyvetta said that one word like it was explanation enough, and Petula nodded as if she fully understood.

"My sweetie is the same damn way. Let me take it off for you with some of this cleansing tonic, as soon as I get settled, and we'll see what we got." She ran her fingers expertly over the hardened cream on Wyvetta's face and then went back to the storeroom where there was a momentary jingle and rattle of glass jars. In a few minutes, she came back with a bottle of orange liquid that she carefully applied to Wyvetta's face in swift even strokes with cotton balls, and the smell of oranges filled the room. "Just relax now and close your eyes," she said in a soothing voice, and Wyvetta, glad for once to be receiving services instead of delivering them, took a deep breath and closed her eyes.

Petula worked quickly and evenly as she stroked the cleanser on Wyvetta's face. I tried to think of a smooth way to find out anything I could about that condo that Tyrone Mason had lived in. Finally I just asked her.

"Wyvetta mentioned that you are from Bloomington?"

"Yup. Been there all my life. Ever want to know anything about Bloomington if you're investigating something, you can give me a call."

"Thanks, Pinky, I'll remember that. Ever hear of a place called the Splendor—"

"Splendid Towers?" Petula put the cotton ball down, and a pleasant, dreamy smile spread across her face. "They're beautiful!"

"That's it," Wyvetta said. "That's what he called them, the Splendid Towers. That was where the fool lived."

"What fool, Wyvetta?" Petula looked puzzled.

"Take one of these doughnuts, Pinky. There are plenty here. Tamara brought them over for us this morning," Wyvetta said, making sure Petula was paid in some small way for the information she was about to give, even though she had no idea she was giving it.

"So it's a nice place?"

"Nice isn't the word for it," Pinky said as she took another cotton ball and dabbed it under Wyvetta's eyes. "Splendid! They really are splendid."

"They're new?"

"State-of-the-art. Everything is splendid!" She obviously liked the word.

"Do you know how much they rent for?"

She thought for a moment. "You can't get nothing in them for under a thousand a month," she said. "Are you interested in renting there?"

"No, not me. A very close friend of mine." Wyvetta caught my eye in the mirror and rolled hers.

"If you want me to find out definitely, let me know. My boyfriend has a friend who manages it, and I know he can get you in. That man is kind of sweet on me, too. He'll do anything I want him to. Men ain't nothing but kids," she added with a wink, and she and Wyvetta both laughed. I could see how she fit right in.

Munching on what I promised myself would be my last doughnut,

I left with a gift bottle of strawberry cleansing lotion, Pinky's number, and her promise to give me a complimentary facial. When I got upstairs, I plugged my kettle in for some tea, turned on my computer for my obligatory fifteen-minute wait, and began to jot down some notes, naming my file NN for Nasty Note. I stared at the blank screen for a while and then in capital letters typed the names of all the people who were directly or indirectly connected with the case and then wrote what I knew about each of them. I don't know why this procedure always helps me, but it does. Maybe it's just seeing the names on the screen and being forced to think about that person for a moment so that my subconscious can do its work. It's the way I organize my thoughts and figure out my next move.

I took out the note and examined it again. *Movin' on up.* The letters were printed on paper with an uneven, torn edge to it, as if it had been ripped from a note pad. The writing, made with a red-inked marker, was sloppy and careless, as if written by a child or somebody trying to disguise his or her handwriting. Everything about the note seemed spur-of-the-moment, the words themselves taken from a rerun TV show from the 1970s that had buried its way into somebody's subconscious.

TYRONE MASON. I stared at the first name, thinking about what I now knew about him: He had been blackmailing Mandy Magic. He probably had a partner, who may have been but more than likely was *not* responsible for his death. I also was reasonably sure that Mandy Magic was using me to smoke him or her out, which meant that partner was probably someone close to her, which said she didn't want to go to the cops unless she was absolutely sure she had it right. She also didn't want to risk putting her business in the street. If Tyrone had been murdered in a random killing like the cops said he had, then that person—whoever she or he was—had simply written the note to torment Mandy Magic. But why?

PAULINE. *A bitch on wheels,* I typed my first impression of her. But she knew Mandy Magic "back when." What were her real feelings about her? What insight and information would she be able to offer about the others? I copied her and all the other home addresses and telephone numbers from my notebook and then, while I was thinking about it, called her office and set up an appointment. She agreed to meet me on Friday night and seemed strangely willing, almost eager, to talk.

KENTON DANIELS III. Was he Mandy's lover? I couldn't get a sense of him at all. I did know he needed money But why would he want to frighten her, unless there was more to their relationship than met the eye? What had been in that strange, sly look that Taniqua had tossed him the day we met? Was she playing with fire and not knowing it?

TANIQUA. I felt a sense of sadness and apprehension as I wrote down her name. She was eighteen years old, legally an adult, but as anyone who has raised a teenager knows, maturity does *not* come with age. What had Tyrone Mason really meant to her? And what about Kenton Daniels? Did she know how dangerous a man like that could be?

MANDY MAGIC. The answer to who she was lay with Starmanda Jackson. It was Starmanda Jackson who had whispered girlish secrets and kissed her first boy in the empty halls of the Hayes Homes. Starmanda Jackson was the one who had learned to fight and cuss and who smoked her first cigarette and turned her first trick. No matter how hard she fought her, Starmanda Jackson would never let Mandy Magic go.

Finally there was RUFUS GREENE. Had be been Tyrone Mason's silent partner, this man who had once been able to take the measure of a woman's soul and sell it like a vial of crack?

Why had she let him back into her life?

I settled back to sip my tea with that question on my mind.

CHAPTER FIVE

"I WAS ALWAYS THE GOOD ONE, BUT SHE HAD ALL THE FUN," Pauline Reese said with a cackle. "You ever have a friend like that? Who does everything they tell you *not* to do and still ends up on top? Now don't get me wrong, I love the girl. She is my best friend, always has been, but she never loses. She always wins."

"Nobody *always* wins."

"Starmanda does." Pauline took out a flask trimmed in black leather and gold and poured a corner of scotch into a narrow water glass. She shook it around as if it contained mixer and ice, took a healthy swallow, and then tossed me a guilty glance.

"I'm not a lush, if that's what you're thinking. It's Friday. I'm tired. I need a drink. It's been a rough week, and I'll be here late." I could hear the bone-tiredness of a woman who works too long and hard in her voice. I knew the feeling.

"I could use one myself," I said with all honesty, as I thought about my week. She didn't need much of an excuse to pour about an inch into a glass for me. I took a polite sip figuring a nip or two at the end of the day, as Wyvetta would put it, couldn't do any harm. There's also nothing like a shared flask to bring out somebody's truth. Pauline leaned back, polished off the remaining liquor in her glass, and poured another generous splash.

We were sitting in the small office to the right of Mandy Magic's large one. Except for the fancy flask on the cluttered desk, the office was as dull, plain, and efficient as the woman who worked in it. Even the telephone was one of those old-fashioned numbers, with a squat body and long twisted cord, which hung over the edge of her desk in a sloppy loop. There was none of the luxury that marked Mandy Magic's space. Gray cotton upholstery instead of red brocade; A&P water glasses instead of Limoges cups; a blue china vase filled with pencils rather than Waterford crystal filled with lilies.

Pauline was dressed in a muddy brown suit trimmed in white. Her hair was poorly styled in a plain, no-nonsense cut, which made me wonder what a day in the Biscuit would do for her. Unlike her high-flying boss, with her Chanel suit, ruby ring, and stylish hair, Pauline Reese was a woman who seemed most at ease in the background.

I had sensed a steely hardness about her on Monday—a hostile edge. She seemed looser tonight. I wondered if it was the liquor. Despite what she'd said, the slur of her words and slight dip of her left eye told me she'd probably been sipping on and off for the better part of the day. She looked nervous when I'd come in and pointedly locked her closed office door after I'd sat down, even though I'd firmly closed it when I'd come in.

"Nothing scares me much," she said with a lift of her head when I asked her about it.

"Except being in an empty office late at night by yourself," I corrected her, and she gave me a conceding smile. I rambled on for a moment or two about crime statistics, break-ins, and the need for security systems while I shuffled around in my bag searching for my notebook. When I didn't feel it, I realized I must have left it on the hood of my car. I'd placed it down when I'd put a ninety-minute tape into the expensive, voice-sensitive tape recorder I'd just purchased and turned on before I'd come upstairs. I'd tucked it into a corner of my bag, on top of my wallet and makeup case, and set my open bag on the desk slightly in front of us, praying that the device was strong enough to pick up our voices. I was reasonably sure that the person Mandy Magic had hired me to find was somebody close to her, and I'd need undeniable proof when I eventually found out. I don't particularly like recording interviews without a person's knowledge, but I was sure that Pauline, or for that matter Kenton or Taniqua, wouldn't want me taking notes. I was also sure that one of the three of them would give me the information I needed.

"If you're looking for a notebook, don't bother," Pauline said, sensing what I was poking around for and holding up her hands in protest. "I don't want anything written down."

"No problem," I smiled agreeably and folded my hands in my lap. Well, nothing would be *written* down. I took a quick sip of my drink, and she matched me—swallow for sip. Bad for her. Good for me.

That first question is always the one that shapes the interview, and I remembered that as I leaned toward her as if she were the most interesting person in the world. I knew that she was the power behind Mandy Magic's throne—or at least that was how she saw herself. But that kind of power rarely gets its due, which always brings resentment. Her resentment was what I knew I needed to get to.

"Could I say something before we begin?" I pasted a saccharine-sweet smile on my lips as I tried to butter her up. "I have to say how much I admire you."

"Me?" she looked surprised and doubtful at the same time.

"Yes. This is such an incredible business—the radio show, the business end, the contracts, Ms. Magic's personal business, and I have to say you seem to handle it all with such aplomb."

"Thank you," she said, still doubtful. "You do the best you can."

"Can you tell me a little about yourself?"

"About myself?" Alarm and suspicion popped out on her face, which told me I'd asked the wrong question; she probably felt that without Mandy Magic there was very little Pauline Reese. "Didn't you come here this evening to talk about Starmanda?" I kicked myself for starting out wrong.

"What did you mean before when you said she was the bad one and you were the good one?" I got back to her point.

"Let's get it straight. I didn't say she was the bad one. I said she had all the fun."

"And fun means?" According to Mandy, her young life had been anything but fun. Pauline thought for a moment before she answered, running her hand over the rim of the glass of scotch as if it she were caressing it. Her voice was hesitant when she replied. She picked her words carefully. "Everything you tell me will be confidential," I added as if she needed it.

"Right!" she said sacarcastically. "I wasn't born yesterday."

"All I want to find out is who is responsible for the note that has alarmed her so much. I'm not interested in anything else, and I assume you didn't write it." *Like she would tell me if she had.*

"I don't resent Starmanda, and I never have," she said after a moment, guessing what I was thinking. "But Starmanda told me to talk to you, so here I am." She took a sip of the drink. "It's hard to get anything out of her, isn't it?"

"Ms. Magic? Yes it is."

"She slams shut parts of her life like doors. She even keeps me out. Well, she hired you against my better advice. She asked for it, so here it is." There was a restrained delight in her voice as she began to speak, an odd kind of relish that surprised me and at the same time made me uncomfortable. She was enjoying this, and that told me something right there. "I'm three years older than she is, always three years ahead of her in school, but she was very smart, always old for her age, always ahead of herself. We met in grammar school. We were both smart, but my mama pushed me in ways that her foster mother, Mrs. Mason, never did."

"So she wasn't brought up by her mother. The one who named her."

"No. Her real mother died when she was young. Her name was Irma Jackson. Her father just kind of disappeared the way men like that do. Starmanda never really knew what happened to her or to him. She was in the system for a while, and then she was taken in by Mr. and Mrs. Mason."

I remembered somewhere in the past reading that she had been a foster child, but as with most things in Mandy Mason's life, there had been more gossip than real information. No concrete facts. No trails to follow. Pauline poured another corner into her glass; she obviously didn't like it dropping below a certain level. "The Masons didn't give a shit about her, if you want to know the truth. If you want to know the truth, nobody gave much of a shit about her except me."

"Do you think that's why she now reaches out to kids in need?" I'd read that somewhere too, that her "tragic childhood," as the article had put it without mentioning much else, was why she cared so much about the helpless—the severely retarded toddler, the orphaned teenager, her own adopted daughter, Taniqua.

"What most people don't understand about Starmanda is that she has always had a golden heart. She is genuinely good-hearted. I've never known a kinder person."

"What about her father's people?" Despite what Pauline had said, I knew that "men like that" usually don't just disappear. Many men feel as connected to children as women, and that love will defy any stereotype you throw its way. Men nurture and nourish, too; I knew that. And the "men like that" Pauline had mentioned also had mothers, aunts, sisters, grandmothers — and their own male kin, for that matter — who knew that blood was richer than spit and would reach out to a kid just because she had so-and-so's eyes or somebody's chin.

"I don't know. Maybe Mrs. Mason was some distant kin; Starmanda never said. She called them family, ended up calling Harold Mason, Tyrone's father, her cousin, which was why she called Tyrone her second cousin, I guess," she looked frustrated for a moment and shook her head as if making an excuse. "This is all from memory, you know. Me and Starmanda never talk about this stuff. She told me she wanted me to talk to to you, so I'm telling you all this, and it better not go any further than this room," she added as she narrowed her eyes, her gaze threatening.

"I promise you I won't repeat anything you've told me," I repeated, praying the tape recorder wouldn't make some kind of weird mechanical noise. "Do you know anything else about her past?"

"Not much. There wasn't much to know, but there was one thing that Starmanda always knew; she knew she'd be somebody. She always knew that about herself. It's funny how some kids know they're going somewhere else."

Her mother hung her spirit on a star.

"Starmanda has always been a very *present* person, if you know what I mean."

"But her past is catching up with her now, wouldn't you say?"

"Maybe."

"So Tyrone Mason was related to her, at least in her mind. Was she close to his father, her first cousin?"

"They used to hang out some in high school. He was kind of tough, kind of a hoodlum, but they claimed each other as kin, so he kind of looked out for her. Tyrone used that old tie, that and Taniqua, to get to her. That much was clear to me." She paused for a moment, remembering something, and then continued.

"We were inseparable even though she was three years younger than me," she continued. "I got a scholarship in my senior year and went away to school. A small arts and science college in Chicago. She told me when I saw her again that, during that time I was away at school, the Masons threw her out for some reason she never really went into, and she dropped out of school. We met again years later. She was making a name for herself at the station by then, and I'd been hired as an office manager."

"What year was that?"

"Around 1974. The owner of the station—white guy, very rich, very old—liked her and looked out for her. Elmer H. Brewster, that was his name. God, I haven't said that man's name in twenty years. We used to laugh about him, call him Elmer Fudd behind his back. He looked a little like Elmer Fudd, too, all doofus and unsure of himself. But he was rich, and they used to say he liked black women. He's dead now.

"It galled me at the time. Me going to school for four years, her only having her GED, and I come back and she's *my* boss. I guess she really came up through the ranks."

On her back? a catty voice within me chimed. "So basically you didn't see her from the time you left her in high school, which was about when, mid-1960s, until you saw her again in the mid-1970s?"

Pauline paused for a moment as if counting the numbers in her head. "Yeah, that's about right. I left for school in 1966. Starmanda had just turned fifteen. There were those three years between us, but we were close. When we met as kids, I knew two things about Starmanda Jackson. I knew we would always be friends. Soulmates. Except she was wild and pretty with that long black hair always hanging down her back and me—" she shrugged. "Nothing much has changed. And I knew she would be somebody just like she said she would be. She would never let anything or anybody stand in her way."

"Do you have any idea what she did while you were away at

school?" I asked like I didn't know what can happen to pretty young girls who think going places means riding down the block in some pimp's Lincoln. "That must have been from the late sixties until you met again in the seventies."

"She doesn't talk about those years much."

"Ever hear her mention a guy named Rufus Greene?"

"No," she said too quickly, and I should have pushed for more.

"Do you have any idea who would want to frighten her now? Maybe somebody from those early years at the station, who resented the way she, uh . . . made her way to the top?" Pauline shrugged that she didn't. "Except for you, were her friends in high school college-bound?"

"There were always boys around her. Men have always liked her. Even now. But for the most part, they were little gangsters. She always seemed to like boys with a dangerous edge." I cringed when she said it, as I thought about my own marginal tastes in men in high school. Save for the presence of my tough, often overbearing big brother, I could have ended up on the block.

"And none of these young hoods stand out in your mind?" I asked, knowing even as I did that high school was probably too far back to go. I wouldn't recognize half the kids from my junior class in high school if they walked past and slapped me across the butt.

She thought for a moment. "I can't think of anybody who would want to get even with her after all these years. To write a weird note? It's too penny-ante. Why try to mess with her mind after all these years? We were all kids then. It must be somebody more recent, somebody she just developed a relationship with who has reason to resent her. Who else would have access?" I sensed she was leading me to Kenton, and I took the hint.

"So what can you tell me about Kenton Daniels III?"

She smiled a sly smile. "What would you like to know?"

"What kind of relationship do the two of them have?"

"Another thing in her life she doesn't talk to me about. But as far as I can see, he uses her for her money, and she for some strange reason seems to need him to fulfill some need of hers. I find the relationship perplexing."

"How did she meet him?"

"Some charity something or other given by some high-class women's group that was honoring her. She originally hired him as a consultant. Her office," she gave a nod to the right, "with all that fancy furniture, the house — that's all Kenton Daniels with his fancy, pretentious self. That's not Starmanda. He bills himself as a 'personal consultant,' whatever the hell that means." She rolled her eyes, and we shared a chuckle at Kenton's expense as she poured us both another inch of liquor. I was beginning to like her better. Or maybe it was the scotch.

"How long have they been together?"

"About a year, I guess. They don't live together. He has his own place. I'm not sure when the professional consultant thing slipped over into the personal, but when it did, she started listening more to him, and that's not good for her."

Or you, I thought. Pain had flickered in her eyes before she dropped them to her desk.

"What kind of relationship do you have with Kenton Daniels?"

She screwed up her mouth in disgust. "We can't stand each other. We've made no secret of our feelings. Most people know it. It's hard to hide it when you don't get along with somebody. I was better at hiding it than he was." She shrugged in the general direction of the office next to hers. "But we work for the same woman. That's his office. He had a gym put in. Mandy did it for herself, she said, but he mainly uses it. He comes in here anytime he feels like it, like this is his office, working out, lifting weights, using those machines.

"And that makes you angry?"

"I don't care one way or the other. Tyrone used to work out with him sometimes," she added as an afterthought. "In the office and in this gym they both go to across town. Somewhere near Belvington Heights, over there where Kenton lives. The two of them were always carrying gym bags with the name of it printed on them. Gandy's Gym, something like that."

"Sounds like Kenton Daniels and Tyrone Mason were pretty tight."

She thought for a moment before she answered. "You would see them out together for drinks, laughing, kidding around. They got along okay. They both belonged to that gym, like I said before."

"Did you know that Tyrone Mason was blackmailing Ms. Magic?" She didn't look surprised.

"About what?"

"I couldn't tell you." I avoided her eyes, afraid I'd somehow betray the shaky trust that Mandy Magic had put in me. "Do you think Kenton could have known about the blackmail? Were they that close?"

The smile on her face was calculating and slow coming, as if Pauline knew more than she was willing to say. "They shared a lot of things, I'll tell you that much. Nothing about the relationship those two had would surprise me. They both did seem to care about Taniqua, though. Tyrone seemed to idolize her, the way she looked. Always playing around with her hair, telling her what to wear, like she was some kind of baby doll or something. Kenton was close to her because Tyrone was. The whole thing struck me as bizarre.

"I don't trust Taniqua and I never have, even though she's young. And despite what Starmanda says—that she reminds her of herself— Taniqua is nothing like Starmanda. She doesn't have the kind of sweetness Starmanda had."

"But Taniqua loved Tyrone, and she seemed to be devastated when he was murdered."

"Seemed to be. You can never tell with Taniqua. She's sneaky, sly. Nothing but a product of her environment. I don't understand what warped sense of sympathy would make Starmanda reach out to a girl like that, but Starmanda is a very powerful woman, and she can do anything she sets her mind to," she added with a look that I wasn't sure was complimentary and that begged me to ask her for more.

"Usually people adopt younger children, not a teenager like that."

"She wanted Taniqua, and she got her. She never told me why, what kind of special magic that kid held for her."

"Do you know anything about her background?"

She leaned back in her chair, poured a splash of scotch into my glass and the remainder into her own. She stared moodily into space for a moment, as if she were contemplating whether or not to answer. "I found out she killed a man. Taniqua, with that pretty angel face of hers. She killed her mother's boyfriend. Killed him. And once you've tasted blood, had that first kill, nothing means anything anymore. Once a murderer, always a murderer, as far as I'm concerned."

I took in a breath when she said it, stunned as I always am by the notion of children who kill. But I was also struck by Pauline's hardness, the cold contempt in the woman's eyes. "That's a very harsh judgment of a very young girl," I finally said. "What were the circumstances?"

"They called it self-defense. She didn't have a father, so they put her in the system for a while. Just like they did Starmanda. Juvenile detention. She was young when she did it, maybe twelve or thirteen. Records were sealed, so I couldn't find out too much, and Starmanda never told me much."

"Maybe she saw something in Taniqua nobody else saw."

"You can take the child out the ghetto, but you can't take the ghetto out the child."

Her words were tossed out lightly, but they dug deeper into me than they should have. I tried not to let it show, but I wondered how true those words were of me and even of Mandy Magic. If she'd thought she would turn me against the kid, she didn't know who I was and where I came from.

"I think that's all." My tone was short, and I didn't mind if my irritation showed. I'd had just enough scotch on an empty stomach not to give a damn one way or the other. I'd also gotten all I was probably going to get from her. She looked surprised and then disappointed.

"That's all?"

"That's it," I said and stood, but she reached across her desk and touched my wrist, as if to keep me from leaving.

"There is one thing more I'd like to tell you," she paused dramatically for emphasis.

"And what is that?"

"That Starmanda Jackson has been my life." She spoke as if it were a confession, holding me in her gaze as if she were giving me some message she dared not say out loud.

Is she in love with the woman? I wondered. *And if she is, what lengths will she go to try to protect that love?* I studied her face, trying to read the message between her words, but she turned quickly back to her work. She was the one who was cutting me off now.

I clicked off the tape recorder as soon as I got out of her office and into the elevator, testing it to see what I'd gotten on the way down. I was eager to settle down and listen to it more closely, to hear again the nuances and pauses in our conversation, to hear things that I had probably missed.

I was still fiddling around with it as I came into the garage. Johns was on duty again. I gave him another five-dollar tip when I saw that he or maybe one of the other guys he worked with had found my notebook on the hood and thoughtfully placed it on the driver's seat where I would spot it. My father had been older than this man when he died, but there had been that indistinguishable grayness about him too. It was impossible to know how old he was or how tough the roads had been that he'd taken to reach this point in his life.

Defeated.

That was the word that came to mind—everything that my brother, Johnny, had sworn he would never be. And Johnny had never become that. He had burned hot and fast until he finally burned himself out. I thought about Jake for a moment, and about how that kind of defeat would never hover around him. I'd gotten used to seeing sadness in his eyes, but not defeat, never defeat. I remembered how his body had touched Ramona Covington's as they'd left the restaurant. I shifted into first gear and then roughly into second with a vengeance, driving out of the garage and back to my office faster and more aggressively than I should have.

He had said he wanted to talk to me sometime today about what was troubling him when I'd seen him Monday, and that had settled somewhere in the back my mind for most of the week. I'd forced myself not to call him. But when the phone rang as I was coming into my office, I knew who it was, and I rushed to get it.

"Tamara." I felt that quick thrill I always did whenever he said my name. "What are you doing there so late? I didn't think I'd catch you."

"Coming back from an interview. Needed to make some notes," I said as briskly and businesslike as I could, snapping on my computer and settling back in my chair to wait.

"I was thinking I might stop by for a minute or two, if it's okay. I just wanted to run this by you. Something I've been running around in my head. If you don't have anything else to do." He sounded uneasy. Nervous. Something I'd never heard in Jake's voice before.

"If you want to. Sure."

"You sound distant, Tamara. Like something's bothering you." He could read me as well as I could read him.

"It's nothing. I'm just tired."

"Tired of me calling you about nothing, huh?"

I smiled despite myself. "You never call about nothing, Jake. Come on by if you want to. I'll be here for a while. What's going on?"

He paused for a moment. There was the familiar despair in his voice. "Phyllis is fine. Denice is okay, too." He said it quickly and his voice sounded better. I could imagine the way his eyes lit up. "Half an hour or so?"

"That sounds good."

I sat for a while after he'd hung up, remembering what we'd talked about when I saw him last, and wondered if I should ask him about his relationship with Ramona Covington. It was funny when I thought about it, how I could be so honest with him about nearly everything in our lives except this. We had once crossed that line that separates passionate and friendly love. One night, shortly after I left my ex-husband, Jake had been comforting me as he always did. This time DeWayne had done something that was particularly galling. My ex-husband lied to me continuously, and I was almost used to it. But he had made a promise to Jamal and broken it with scarcely a thought. I had seen the sadness come into my son's eyes the way it always did into mine, and that, on top of everything else, was more than I could take. Jake held me close to him when I started to cry. I still remember the strength of his body and how comfortably I eased into him. He kissed my forehead and then my lips lightly, just a trace of a kiss, but a thrill as intense as anything I'd ever known had gone through me. We stopped quickly, then touched again, embraced, as I brought my body into his with a sensation that overwhelmed me. I knew he felt it too. We backed away, both of us unwilling to acknowledge that moment. Yet even now I knew that he hadn't forgotten it, that we could renew it with a touch that lingered longer than it should. We know ourselves too well, how deeply we can love or hurt each other. Passion is a risky thing; once it's cut loose, there's no telling what it will create or destroy in its wake. I turned off my computer without typing any notes. Then I went to the small refrigerator and got out a bottle of Deer Park water, poured it into my tea kettle, and waited for it to boil.

Would anything be worth that risk?

I wondered again. I couldn't forget the apprehension I'd felt when I watched him walk out of that restaurant with another woman. Something within me had changed.

Sooner or later you had to pay the band what it was due.

I went to the restroom down the hall, rinsed out two cups, and returned to my office, locking the door behind me and thinking for a moment of Pauline Reese. Empty offices were spooky at night, especially this one, even though darkness hid some of the more glaring problems.

I pulled down the shades when I came back in, and the overhead bulb, which seemed less harsh at night, gave the room a surprisingly mellow glow that hid the various rips and stains on the worn grayish-brown carpet. I poured some water from the Deer Park bottle onto my orphan aloe plant; I felt guilty that it needed repotting. Its mottled color and the various winding tendrils now sprouting from the battered pot brought to mind alien vegetation from a 1950s horror movie. I picked off a leaf and broke it, and clear liquid oozed onto my hands. Telepathically I promised the plant I'd take it home to pamper and repot it as soon as I got some time.

The kettle whistled, and I poured boiling water into one of the cups, sorted through my Celestial Seasonings tea assortment and settled on Lemon Mist; it was too late in the day for the tart boost of Red Zinger. I needed something mellow. As the lemon fragrance floated up from my cup, I thought again about Mandy Magic and Pauline Reese. They had been girls together, as a great writer once put it, and that brought its own brand of responsibility, loyalty, and love.

Could Pauline's unrequited love be responsible for that note? Was that love actually the source of the antagonism between her and Kenton, and was that the real reason for her hostility toward Taniqua? They had both replaced her in her best friend's—love object's—affection. Maybe this was her warped way of getting even. But how deep could it go? Those small acts of vandalism that Mandy had mentioned at our first meeting; had they been secret rage secretly expressed? Would there be another note, more threatening, more hostile?

I knew now that it had been a smart move for me to record the interview, if for no other reason than to get Pauline's true feelings about Kenton and Taniqua down on tape. Mandy Magic would not want to believe that her oldest friend could have such animosity toward two people whom she cared deeply about. She wouldn't want to think that Pauline's hidden anger might have led her to write a note that she knew would frighten and alarm her. Could it have been a momentary weakness? Pauline obviously drank more than a little bit; maybe she'd been drunk when she'd vandalized the car and office door or written that note. I regretted not asking her about *her* relationship with Tyrone Mason and not pushing her about Rufus Greene. I'd have to talk to her about that later. What else had I missed?

Mandy Magic was a survivor, and I suspected she found loyalty more important in her friends and colleagues than anything else. I suddenly felt sad for Pauline Reese, and sorry that I and my hidden tape recorder would be the instrument of her downfall. What would happen to her when Mandy knew the truth about her feelings? And Mandy would have to know.

Jake's loud knock interrupted my thoughts.

"Tamara, that lock on the door downstairs is broken again. You should tell Annie to have another locksmith take a look at it," he said with concern in his voice after I unlocked the door and let him in. He was dressed in his lawyer uniform: pinstripes, wing tips, striped suspenders, the whole package. I could see a week's worth of fighting for justice in the weary way he dropped his muscular frame into his chair.

"Got some more of that? I could probably use something stronger, though, considering the kind of week I've had."

"Unless we break into the Biscuit and steal some of that Johnnie Walker Red Wyvetta's always talking about, Lemon Mist is going to have to do it," I said as I poured him a cup.

"Thanks."

"It's just tea."

"Not for the tea. For everything. Always. For letting me come by like this. For—"

"Oh, for God's sake, Jake, shut up!" I snapped, surprised myself at the irritation in my voice. I realized suddenly that I was annoyed with him for taking me for granted. His eyes were hurt when he glanced at me. "We look out for each other, Jake," I said in a softer voice. "You do things for me—I do things for you. You know that."

He studied me warily for a moment and nodded that he understood, but I knew he had no idea. We talked for a while as we always did, about Jamal, Denice, everything but Ramona Covington. Finally he told me why he had come by.

"I've been thinking about sending Denice away to school, that maybe she should be away from Phyllis, from what is happening to our lives, from me."

That was a surprise and my face showed it. "Like a boarding school or something like that?" I asked, not sure for a moment what he was talking about. The idea of sending a kid away to school was something that was completely foreign to me, something rich white folks—and rich black folks too, these days—did with their kids when they didn't want to be bothered with them. Not Jake Richards. I studied him for a few moments. Not sure what to think. "Because of Phyllis?"

"That's one reason." I watched him, knowing what the other reason was.

"And the other reason?"

"I hinted about it at lunch." He studiously avoided my eyes. "I think she needs to get away from me, to expand her world, meet some new challenges."

"And you need to get away from her?"

"No." The hurt rose again in his eyes. "You know how I love that girl."

"I'm not questioning that, Jake. But you want my honest advice? Why don't you be honest with yourself? No. I don't think you should send her away."

I was sure now of the answer to the question that had been on my mind for the last few days. "I think you have to resolve things for yourself first. For yourself and for your daughter. Don't think by sending her away to some boarding school that you will somehow make anything better. For her or for you."

"For me?" he looked genuinely puzzled.

"Aren't you sleeping with Ramona Covington?" It was a statement asked like a question, and he sank back into his chair, his mouth slightly opened in surprise as if I had slapped him.

"I don't think that's any of your business." He got it together quickly and his voice was solemn when he answered me. I sank back into *my* chair then, knowing on some level that he was right, and not sure what to say or do about it. We sat still, avoiding each other's eyes, listening to the creaks of the old building for a while and then to the sound of the cars outside the window. Neither of knew where to take it from there. I didn't like the silence in the room or what it meant.

"It's not fair to Denice to send her to a school so you won't have to deal with your guilt."

"I don't feel guilty about anything. I've just been under some pressure, I'm not sure—"

"And Ramona Covington is a quick easy way to relieve some pressure?"

"I didn't say that."

"Of course you did. Who do you think you're kidding?"

"Tamara, don't take it—"

"Take it where? You're sleeping with her, right? Never mind what that says about her. The question is: What does it say about you?" I was riding my high-morals horse and enjoying it. But anger had tightened my throat, and my body felt hot. I couldn't trust my voice, so I picked up my cup filled with lemon-flavored tea and made myself sip it. I looked cool and in control, but my hand was trembling.

"Don't bring Ramona into this. Nothing is the way it sounds. It's not that complicated, Tamara. We—she—" He paused as if searching for words. I filled them in for him.

"She what—doesn't mean anything? She is just somebody you fuck? And you know I don't use that word unless that is what it is being done, and that is pretty much what is being done, isn't it?"

"Tamara, we shouldn't be talking about this."

"You're right." I wasn't trying to disguise my anger anymore. I was angry at him and angry at myself for being such a hypocrite, knowing on some level that I wished it were me. But it wasn't. "I guess, you're right, about it being none of my business. There is nothing between us. Not really." I took a breath with those words, stood up, went to the window, avoided his eyes.

"That's not true, and we both know it."

I turned to face him. "But why Ramona? Oh, I just remembered! How did you put it before? That you knew there was nothing that you could ever do or say that would ever really hurt her?"

He dropped his eyes down to the tea in the cup on the desk before him.

"Do you really believe that, Jake? That you can use somebody like that? That there is any woman in the world who is that hard, that tough?" Even as I said it, I couldn't believe I was actually defending the honor of Ramona Covington, but I was, and with it my own honor, and that of every other woman whose strength had been mistaken for invulnerability.

"Tamara, what do you expect me to say to you?"

"Tell me the truth, Jake. Just tell me the goddamn truth."

The phone rang and I let it ring, not caring who it was or what they wanted. Karen at my answering service would get it after the fourth ring, and I'd call her later on. Nothing at this moment was as important as this. Whoever it was hung up and then called back five minutes later. I reached for it as it stopped ringing for the second time.

"You know how I feel about you," he said when the room was silent.

"I don't know anything."

"This has nothing to do with our relationship, our bond, Tam. You know that."

"So you *are* sleeping with her then."

"If I were, would you be angry for Phyllis or for yourself? Why don't *you* be honest for a change?"

I thought about it for a moment. "Okay. I'll be honest. For both of us." But it wasn't for both of us, and I knew it. *Should I have slept with him? Should I now? What has kept me from it?* I answered that last question in my mind: It was because I knew that everything would change forever if I did, and there was no telling what would be left in its place. It was because we were safe like this, and that was what both of us had accepted in silent gratitude. *But what had we given up?* It wasn't Phyllis who was hurting now; it was me, and even as I attacked him, I had to face the truth that I was too much of a coward to admit it. But so was he.

"I'm not going to talk about this anymore." He sounded lost and unsure of himself, and I couldn't remember the last time I'd heard that in his voice. Yet there was a finality, too, that made me glance away from him, knowing I could push him no further. This was, he decided, his business, not mine, and there was nothing I could do about it. "Tamara, I've never asked you about your business. I've never let anything like this interfere with our relationship. And I know there have been many men—"

"*Many* men?" I asked incredulously, and the mood in the room lightened.

"Well, some . . . maybe one." He smiled, half-joking, and for that moment our connection was back. But just for that moment.

"One or two hundred. However many, it's none of your damn business," I cut my eyes, my voice dangerously close to childish.

"I know that better than you do, but the important one, what's his name?"

Basil Dupre. I didn't say his name, but I certainly thought it. Basil

Dupre is the one man in my life who has always been able to turn my self-restraint and good sense into mint jelly. Even in the midst of an argument with Jake, the thought of the man in all his fine, sensual glory, brought a smile of guilty pleasure to my lips. I took a sip of tea, letting the cup conceal my smile from Jake, and avoided his eyes. He answered the question for me.

"I never have asked about that man, and you know how I feel about men like that, and I never will ask you." He was on his high horse now, but a smile, very slight, formed on his lips. I wasn't sure for a moment whether to smile back or smack his face. "And if I did—if I had the nerve to ask you about him, grill you about this . . . uh . . . come-what-may, ongoing relationship you have with this man that at its best is a mistake and at its worst damn-right dangerous—what would you tell me?"

"I'd tell you the truth," I said, but he knew I was lying.

"Couldn't you find anyone better than Ramona Covington?" I swung the conversation back to surer ground.

"Tamara, I've told you. I'm not going to say anything else about Ramona. This is all *your* assumption."

"And I shouldn't assume?"

"I don't have to do this anymore." He sounded like the child now, and then he paused for a moment, collecting his breath, his thoughts. "I don't want things to change between us, Tamara. You and Jamal are too precious to me. And I know how you feel about my wife and my daughter."

"Have you ever thought about how Ramona Covington might feel about that wife and daughter?" I sounded like a prosecuting attorney. I didn't care.

"They don't concern her."

"Jake, you're a fool," I said, my voice quiet and matter-of-fact, but I meant it and he knew it. He dropped his head. I didn't give a damn.

"Tamara, you know what you mean to me."

"I'm not sure anymore."

We sat there for a while longer. He cleared his throat, pointedly glanced at his watch. It was time for him leave, and we both knew it because neither of us knew what else there was to say. He stood up. I stared at my empty cup. "So what are you going to do about Denice?" I asked him, still not looking at him.

"I don't know yet."

I glanced up, a nasty smirk on my face. "Just don't let your dick do your thinking for you." He visibly cringed.

"You know the truth about us, Tamara."

"And just what is that truth, Jake? Why don't you tell me?"

When he spoke, there was a tenderness in his voice that I couldn't remember hearing except when he talked about his daughter. "That it would be impossible to hold anything back if I made that kind of commitment to you, the kind you deserve. That I couldn't sidestep with you, cheat you out of anything. Everything I have I would have to give to you, and I can't and will not do that now. Have you *really* thought what that would cost us both? How destructive it could end up being?"

"And Ramona, what do you owe her"

He gave a slight smile. "Some discretion."

"Just leave, please."

"We're not finished."

"As far as I'm concerned, we are."

"I'll call you?"

"I don't think so."

He nodded as if he understood and closed the door behind him, turning the knob twice to make sure it was locked when he left. I got up to watch him from the window as he walked to his car without looking back. My heart was pounding, and my throat was so tight I knew I could hardly swallow. I packed up my things and headed back home, too.

Jamal was spending the night with a friend, so the house was empty and silent when I got home. It was also cold—the furnace was on one of its frequent vacations. But it was a relief in a way; it gave me a way to get Jake and Ramona off my mind. I tinkered with it until I got it relit and then found a can of soup—Goya's black bean—and made a tuna fish sandwich and ate it as I watched something mindless on the TV in the kitchen. I forced myself to stay up until eleven, and then scoured the tub with Comet, poured in a capful or two of some bubble bath I'd picked up at The Body Shop, and filled the tub to its limit with warm water. Then I lit two square bayberry-scented candles, poured myself a glass of chardonnay, put on some CDs by my homegirl Sarah Vaughan, whom I always turn to in times of crisis, and settled back into the fragrant tub to think about his words and what they meant.

I couldn't sidestep with you, cheat you out of anything. Everything I have I would have to give to you, and I can't and will not do that now. Have you really thought what that would cost us both? How destructive it could end up being? I knew he was right, but it didn't lessen my sorrow or the jealousy I felt toward Ramona Covington and what she was free to enjoy. It was as if something very precious that I thought had belonged to me had been taken from me. Yet I had never really owned it, and my claim had been a lie.

When I finally pulled myself out of the tub, my fingers were wrinkled and I was dizzy. I forced myself not to think of him as I dried off quickly, slapped on some lotion and slipped into a satiny nightgown just because I liked the feel of it against my skin. I made my mind blank as I found a copy of a mystery Annie had given me and I'd been trying to make time to read. I settled down in bed with my head propped up on pillows, the TV on, and the book lying open. But I stared off into space, unable to concentrate on either.

Nothing had changed, yet everything had.

I finally drifted off into a fitful sleep, woke back up, turned off the TV, drifted back, and then woke suddenly when I realized the phone was ringing. I glanced at the clock: four A.M. *Jake!* I thought but let it ring, and then wondered if it was the same person who had called me before. I panicked as I realized that it could be about Jamal and reached for it, knocking the phone to the floor and sitting up to retrieve it.

"Who?" I muttered the one word clumsily, not thinking clearly enough to say hello. There was a pause at the other end, and the sound of someone weeping. I sat up straight, fully awake, my heart pounding. "Who is this?"

"Tamara?" It was a woman's voice, strange yet familiar—Mandy Magic's voice. "She's dead. Somebody came in. Broke in maybe, took that stupid old phone she liked to keep around, wound it around her neck like a rope, squeezed the life out of her. Oh, God—" her voice broke off into a moan. "They just told me. They just called me. I'm sorry. I didn't know who else to call. I'm sorry."

"Mandy?" I yelled into the phone, even though I knew who it was, knew whom she was talking about. I had to ask her anyway.

"Who, Mandy, who?"

"My friend, my Pauline." She spoke with all the anguish in the world.

"How do you know?"

"They called me. The cops. Somebody found her. A few hours ago, sitting there in her office, working for me. Somebody took the wire off that phone, they wound it around her neck. Somebody squeezed the life out of her." I held the phone for a moment, unable to speak, and she repeated what she'd said again in the same voice with the same turn of hysteria riding her words, as if forcing herself to believe it.

"Where are you now?"

"I'm at home. They called me. And I heard a noise outside, and I opened my door, and it was on the steps. Waiting for me to come outside, to pick it up." I caught my breath before I asked her.

"Another note?"

"Yes," she finally said, her voice a shadow of itself.

CHAPTER SIX

SO THEY KNEW HOW TO GET TO HER. OR MAYBE THEY HAD *always known.* I advised her to tell the cops everything she knew, starting with the notes that worried her so much. Pauline's death had changed everything, and there was an outside chance that both her murder and Tyrone's were connected. I also warned Mandy that the longer she waited, the more danger she put Kenton and Taniqua in. She finally talked to the police. I was duty-bound to share what I knew too.

But in reality, I didn't have much to offer. The police listened patiently with mild interest to what I had to say then dismissed the two notes as some weird attempt at getting attention from a disgruntled fan and insisted that Tyrone Mason was simply the victim of a band of robbers who preyed on gay men. I knew that they were dismissing his death with the same indifference with which they often dismiss the murders of straight black men and it made me mad, but there was nothing I could do about it. As for the death of Pauline Reese, they were sure she had surprised a thief and been murdered so she couldn't identify him. Besides that, Tyrone was stabbed and Pauline was strangled. Different weapons and different modi operandi more often than not meant different killers with different motives.

Over the next few days, Mandy Magic became increasingly dependent on me, and I couldn't think of a gentle way of discouraging her. Pauline Reese had been her best friend, confidante, and business adviser, and her sudden, violent death left Mandy vulnerable and frightened. There was nobody else around she could lean on for support, so I was forced to fill the bill.

She called me at least fifteen times later that Saturday and the Sunday and Monday after the murder, starting around seven in the morning and continuing to as late as two in the morning. Often she simply needed a comforting word or common-sense advice about what she should do and how she should protect herself. Mostly she rambled, about their childhood, friendship, and what Pauline had meant to her, and how she would not be able to go on without her. I knew that she needed somebody to listen to her grief and tried to offer the best support I could. But from the beginning, I'd had mixed feelings about Mandy Magic. Our "friendship," such as it was, felt both unauthentic and awkward. But recalling how my grandmother used to bring fried chicken, cakes, and macaroni and cheese to grief-stricken families, I knew that sharing grief is one of the things women do for each other, so I put aside my weekend chores and made myself listen to the woman cry. But by the end of each day, I was exhausted.

The cops spent the weekend after the murder and most of Monday combing the crime scene, which they had designated as Pauline's office and the small reception area and narrow corridor that led to it. They took photographs, searched for prints, and questioned all of us — Mandy, me, and what was left of her family. I suggested she call a lawyer and more than once picked up the phone to call Jake, but I always ended up putting it down. I knew sooner or later I'd have to find somebody else.

I've never been comfortable talking to the police, even when I was one of them, but they seemed satisfied with everything I said. I shared with them what Pauline had told me about Kenton and Taniqua, so they became particularly curious about and interested in Kenton Daniels III and the animosity Pauline bore him. The office suite had not been broken into, so the person who killed her must have been let in or had a key. There had also been no sign of forced entry into Pauline's office. Nothing had been disturbed, nothing moved. The only thing taken had been her life. There had been no prints or evidence left. There had been signs that she had left the office for a short time and then come immediately back, but the police weren't sure why she'd gone out or where. One talkative cop, who remembered my brother when I mentioned my last name, did finally share the official version of what they suspected had happened.

According to him, a new construction firm was renovating offices directly above and below Mandy Magic's suite. Although the master keys were not marked as such, they suspected that an unauthorized person had gotten a set. The maintenance and security staff also had duplicates, so it would also have been possible for one of several strangers to gain access to the suite. But they were still puzzled by how the killer had entered her office itself. I'd told the cops how fearful Pauline had seemed that night and that I was certain she had locked her door after I'd left. But she must have unlocked it again, either to talk to someone or check on a noise she'd heard outside.

Mandy Magic had asked the police if she could visit the office on Tuesday morning to sort through her things and pick up some personal files. Her office had been locked when the crime had taken place, and had remained that way, so they didn't have a problem with it. Much to my dismay, she also told them that I was her personal bodyguard and asked permission for me to join her, which they also granted. So I reluctantly pulled my old .38 out of a locked box I keep in my closet at home, strapped it into my shoulder holster, picked out a loose-fitting black pantsuit and black Nike sneakers, and looking like a hit-girl for the Mob, tried to pass myself off as somebody's protector. A dour-looking cop studied me suspiciously when I entered the suite, examining my credentials for so long I didn't think he was going to give them back. Finally, he opened the door and escorted me in.

A straggly piece of yellow tape roped off Pauline's office. I shuddered as I passed it, hardening myself to the scene. I've always believed that buildings and rooms can be as haunted by violent death as people, and there was an eerie stillness about this place, as palpable as a smell. Yet there were few physical signs that violence had occurred. Pauline's chair sat where it had been when I'd last seen her, which meant that she had probably been standing when she was attacked. The phone was gone of course, bagged and marked for evidence like everything else.

Mandy Magic was packing up files when I entered her office; all the old elegance was gone. There were no lilies in the vase, and the shades, as dull and unattractive now as the ones in my office, were pulled down to keep out what little sun there was. The room was stuffy, and the file cabinets were open. Several piles of papers were stacked on her desk. Little more than a week ago, I had sat across from her, sipping coffee and savoring my luck, in awe of her power and fame. But she was broken this morning, and when she spoke it was in a whisper.

"We were a team all her life. For as long as I knew her, we were a team."

Starmanda Jackson has been my life.

"She told me how much your friendship meant to her," I said for the twentieth time in three days, but I knew it brought her comfort and that she would probably never get tired of hearing it. "How is Taniqua coping with all this?" It had occurred to me that in the last three days neither of us had mentioned her.

"She's okay. She's seen a lot of grief in her life. Like me, I guess." I thought about Pauline and her feelings about the girl. "I want to think it's random. The cops think it might have been random. That it wasn't aimed at me personally." She shuffled absentmindedly through her papers and then went to the window, glanced out of it, and sat back down facing me. "It could have been random like that. But people think all kind of stupid things about me, that I keep money packed away in a drawer in my office, that I have more to give than I do. People are resentful, people I don't even know."

Movin' on up.

"Yes," I said. "People can be resentful."

We sat in silence for a moment, both of us listening to the cop down the hall as he opened the door, spoke in a monotone to somebody who had knocked, and then closed it behind him. He knocked on our door and without waiting for an answer glanced inside, his eyes telling us that time was passing and he wanted to go. Mandy gazed around the room, her face anguished, as if she were saying good-bye.

"Did you tell them about the notes?" she asked me.

"They didn't think it meant too much."

"Maybe they're right."

"They feel they've solved Tyrone's murder. They still feel that it was a mugging gone bad. As for Pauline—" Noting her reaction, I reached over and squeezed her hand to reassure her. "They seem to be leaning toward the idea that maybe somebody got hold of the keys from the construction crew and sneaked in, and that Pauline heard a noise, came out to check, spotted somebody, and ran back into her office to call outside. Before she could get help, they think whoever did it snatched the phone out of her hand and in a rage wrapped it around her neck. They seem to think that's what happened."

"And the note, coming like it did right after Pauline's murder?"

"They think it was coincidence. Somebody playing a vicious joke."

"But it came right afterward."

"They think that you were very upset and that you may have gotten the times wrong, or that it was put there the night before. That it was coincidence."

"Like after Tyrone?" She shook her head in disbelief. "Somebody is coming for me," she said quietly, and I could see the fear in her eyes.

"The cop, the older one who was here, wants to talk with Kenton and Taniqua again. Do you have any idea what he's after? If they think it was an attempted robbery, why would they want to talk with them again?"

"Probably routine stuff." I hoped I'd convinced her. The last thing she needed was to worry about them, but I was sure that I hadn't been the only person Pauline had confided in regarding her feelings about the two. I wondered where they had been the previous night, and I asked her finally because I knew the cops would.

"They were together, but I don't know where they were." She looked lost for a moment, and then she threw back her head, pulled in a breath and let it out, pulling some strength from somewhere, getting it together in the space of a minute and a half. I'd seen her do it before, and I admired it.

"You're very close to Taniqua, aren't you?"

"We protect each other."

"Do you mind if I ask you something?"

"What?" Her eyes studied me suspiciously. I thought for a moment about forgetting it but decided to ask her anyway.

"Why did you adopt her, an older, troubled child like that?"

"Because she reminded me of her mother." She glanced toward the door, making sure it was closed. We couldn't hear the cop anymore, but she had spoken in a whisper anyway, and I answered her back that way.

"Are *you* her mother?"

"No. What made you think that?" She'd taken such a long time to answer, for an instant I thought she might be, even though the dates didn't make sense.

"The way you talk about her."

"I love her because I loved her mother."

"Who was her mother?"

"Somebody I knew during my years as a teenage whore. Her name was Theresa." Her words were defiant, almost proud like she dared me to have something to say about it. She settled back in her chair then, and I could tell by the way she stared straight ahead, her eyes slightly unfocused, that she had a tale to tell. She spoke in a monotone, her voice empty of emotion as if she were talking about somebody else.

"We both worked for Rufus Greene. She was about a year older than me, but still young, no more than seventeen. I just hit fifteen when I turned my first trick, stayed with him most of the five years after that, damn near five years. Dropped out for about a year when I was seventeen going on eighteen. Tried to change my life for a minute, but mostly I was with Rufus, working for him. Theresa showed me what she could of the ropes, the kind of thing a seventeen-year-old knows who thinks she knows it all. God, we were young. I think of those bastards who used us like they did, paying a fifteen-year-old kid for sex, and there's no prison low-down and filthy enough to hold them."

"Where would you put Rufus Greene?" I broke in, wondering what low-down, nasty prison she'd save for him. Surprisingly, she only laughed, a scornful, half-amused chuckle.

"He just took advantage of what was already there. It started with boys we knew. We weren't doing it for *real* money then, mostly defying our parents, having that kind of power over boys. Don't you remember the early and mid sixties? Maybe you don't, but it was high times and free sex, drugs, and rock 'n' roll, even for young kids like us.

"Theresa was already on her own by then, living with an older cousin, who was tricking every now and then for Rufus—Bunny, her

name was. Pauline had left for college by then, and I was lonely for a
friend. Theresa used to hang out with Harold, my cousin. We hit it off.
Then when I left home—"

"You ran away?"

"I was one of those toss-away kids nobody gives a good goddamn
about. Yeah, that was me. My stepfather used to bone me on the side
every now and then. While his good wife was screeching away her vocal
chords at choir practice."

She said it as if it meant nothing, as matter-of-fact as if she'd said
he used to take her to the A&P or put her on curfew for getting bad
grades. Nausea swept through me so quickly I felt dizzy for a moment.
But I knew I shouldn't have been surprised. Young girls don't become
whores just to make a couple of bucks. I should have seen and recognized her past more easily. It was in that voice that soothed and com-
forted thousands and in the compassion that made her reach out to
those in need. She had been powerless, too, and she would never let
herself forget it. I felt myself being drawn to her again, reassured by this
new revelation.

"Mandy, you were raped by your stepfather?"

"Old story, isn't it? Yeah," she shrugged offhandedly and smiled in
that way that I'd learned meant she was in more pain than she wanted
you to know. "Yeah, he raped me, but there wasn't a hell of a lot I or
even my Harold could do about it except hold my hand when I cried at
night. We were close then, and he tried to protect me, which is why I
always loved him, but he was just a kid, too. He protected me the best
way he could. But I finally left. Hung around the streets awhile. Lived
with a married guy who had left his wife for a while, then started turning tricks for real. Seemed an easy way to make some money, the only
way a kid has to make enough money to eat and live.

"It was going all right for a while, but then I got raped again by
some old bastard, the same age as my stepfather, can you imagine that?
He slapped me around, liked to slap around little girls, I guess, see them

scared. If he'd tried it a few years later, I would have slit his filthy throat, but I didn't know too much then. It was the first and only time a man took me like that for free. Theresa jumped on him on like a cat, though. Protecting me. She was always protecting me, looking out for me, if a seventeen-year-old girl can look out for one fifteen. And after that night, we decided we needed some help out there on the street, some protection. And Rufus came on the scene to show us how to make a business of it."

"How much older was he than you?"

"A kid, too. Nineteen, maybe? At most he never had more than five girls working for him. Me, Theresa, a little redbone girl named Ruby, one he called Jewel, and Bunny. None of us over eighteen, but I was the youngest. Rufus and the rest of the girls even had a sweet-sixteen party for me when I turned sixteen—all the coke I could snort and drink. Can you imagine that? We weren't nothing but kids."

She leaned back on the chair now, a smile on her lips, as if the telling of this brought back a pleasant memory she hadn't thought of in a while. She lit a cigarette, shaking out the match with a quick, nervous twist of her wrist. She'd been smoking steadily for the past few days now. I could smell it on her clothes and in her hair. Even her voice was hoarse, both from the cigarettes and the crying too, I guess. But there was no bitterness in it now. Her voice was empty, as if all the shame had been cried out of it.

"How did you get out, Mandy?"

"Walked out. With the help of a friend or two. Angels come in devils' clothes sometimes, Tamara. Don't let them fool you," she added, her voice confidential. "Started working for the station. Didn't hear from Rufus again until Taniqua killed that man who had beaten up Theresa."

"So Rufus Greene came to you with Taniqua and said she was Theresa's child and he needed your help." I smelled a rat, and his name was Rufus Greene.

Her voice rose in defense of him when she answered me, as she made her point with clipped words. "No. He didn't come to me. I could look at the girl and see she was Theresa's child. There was no doubt about that. Rufus had been looking out for her from the sidelines. Sending Theresa money to help take care of her. Until Theresa was dead.

"I'd heard about this child who had killed the man who beat and murdered her mother when I was hosting a fundraiser for a battered-women's shelter. My heart had gone out to them both then, but I had no idea who they were until I saw Taniqua. Then I knew exactly whose child she was and what her history must be. Theresa had pulled herself out, too, like I did, but the angels hadn't touched her like they had me. She'd gotten pregnant, had Taniqua, and then ended up like she did. She had the worst luck of any whore I ever knew. I guess I took her share. More than her share. I've always been lucky. Always landing on my feet. Someone told me once it was my mama looking out for me, up there in heaven. Making sure her baby came out all right in the end."

I studied her for a moment, thinking again how many sides there were to this woman, and wondering if finally Pauline's death had cut her defenses away and how maybe now she had nothing more to hide. Or did she?

"How does Rufus Greene fit into all of this?" I was still doubtful.

"He thought he might be Taniqua's father. Theresa was tied to Rufus in ways I wasn't. They were always close. He preferred her and would protect her above any of the rest of us, and we all knew it."

"A pimp and a whore? Mandy, pimps don't usually come with that kind of parenting instinct." I hadn't meant the words to sound as harsh and sarcastic as they had, and I could see by the way she looked at me that she thought they were crueler than they should have been. She dropped her eyes and began stacking folders again.

"I'm sorry," I said.

"You're the first person in twenty years I've told that story to."

"I didn't mean—" She cut me off.

"What do they say, Tamara Hayle? Let him who is without sin cast the first stone? You cast them long and hard, don't you, sister? He has changed. We were kids who knew nothing about nothing and thought we knew it all. I was all of fifteen when I met my first John, and twenty when I met my last—if you can even call him that. Theresa was seventeen going on eighteen, and Rufus, with those flat feet that kept him out of Vietnam, had just turned nineteen himself. He was never much of a pimp, anyway," she added with a dismissive shrug.

"What do you mean?"

"He didn't have the heart for it, that mean hardness that it takes to really pimp somebody right. He wasn't by nature a woman-hater, and we all ran roughshod over him, except for Theresa who actually cared about him. He was just a little hustler with no good sense when he started out, trying to stay alive like everybody else. Hell, I was tougher than he was, and I knew it."

"He looks pretty tough to me."

"Looking tough and being tough are two different things. I could show you the most doe-eyed, baby-faced pimp in the world who could cut your tongue loose from your throat without missing a line of blow. Half the pimps in Newark were after Rufus's women. The other half finally ran him out of town because he wouldn't feed us dope. Theresa went running right behind him."

"And you?"

"I had begun to make my own way by then." She avoided my eyes.

"Pauline mentioned a white guy, rich she said, that looked out for you. I think his name was Elmer Brewster, something like that?" She shot me a look that said she wasn't going there even before she said the words.

"What did she say about him?"

"Not much."

She smiled as if relieved. "And that's what I'm going to say. Not much. The man is dead and gone, so what does it matter?"

"Since he's dead and gone, what *does* it matter?"

Before she could answer me, the cop knocked on the door, and in bodyguard fashion I rose to open it, explaining that we needed a few more minutes to finish up. When I sat back down, Mandy had started going through her files again, looking, I suspected, for nothing in particular, determined to keep herself busy. I watched her for a moment or two before I asked another question.

"Why was Rufus Greene at your house last week when I came by?" She glanced up and then continued smoothing out, tucking in, taking out papers from the folders.

"He was dropping off Taniqua. They'd gone to visit Theresa's grave. She's buried down in South Jersey. The anniversary of her death was last Tuesday, the day you came by the house." There was no emotion in her voice when she explained it. But I thought about Pauline and what she had said about the girl, and a chill bit into my bones.

"That was about two weeks after Tyrone was killed?"

"Yes, I guess so."

"Don't you think that affected her? The anniversary of her mother's death, Tyrone's death, her killing the man she killed. All of them coming so close like that."

"No. Taniqua's life has changed since Theresa died. The records about that man's death are sealed. Nobody ever has to know about it, that it was really her."

"But some people know. Like Pauline. And Rufus Greene."

"Yes. He knows."

"Does she see him often?"

"Often enough."

"And you've told the girl to lie about him and their relationship?"

"Sometimes lying is the only way there is. Don't you even know that yet?" I was used to how quickly she could switch from sweet and generous to bitter and nasty, so her tone and words didn't throw me as much as they had that first day in her house. But I had some words to say today, too, and I was determined to tell her a truth I knew she wouldn't want to hear.

"You've taught her to be liar, Mandy, just like you can be. But do you lie to yourself? Can you tell me that? Do you lie to yourself?"

She got up and turned her back on me, taking folders out of the short wooden file cabinets behind her. I watched her for a while longer and then left without saying good-bye.

"She done in there?" the cop said as I passed him.

"Maybe you should ask her."

"Take it easy, then."

I avoided saying anything to Johns this time out when I got my car from the garage, though I could see from that desperate, begging look in his eyes that expected something from me—either a kind word or a few bucks, but I didn't have either to give. I was too worn out.

I glanced into the Biscuit when I came back into my building, glad that Wyvetta was busy with somebody's head, so I wouldn't have to talk to her, either. I closed my door behind me gently, so she wouldn't hear me, and then just sat at my desk, thinking about Mandy Magic and how lying and avoiding the truth was much of who she had become and what she had said about my casting the first stone. I scolded myself for a while about leaving without saying good-bye. The woman had had a very rough couple of days. But damn it, so had I. Had I never in my life lied about something that made me ashamed?

She'd filled in some missing years for me, though—those between 1966 and 1974, those years when Pauline Reese had disappeared from her life. I had enough new names to add to my list and at least consider. I turned on my computer, pulled up the NN file, and jotted them down: Theresa, Ruby, Bunny, Elmer Brewster, Jewel. *Angels looking like devils*. I wrote that down too.

Who was she talking about?

I didn't have any last names except Brewster's, but maybe there would be a way I could check old arrest records for some of the others. But in the end they would probably simply be names. And except for Rufus Greene, they were probably long gone and best forgotten.

The phone rang again and I picked it up. It was Jamal. A smile broke out on my face.

"Ma?"

"Yeah."

"What time you coming home?" Jamal *never* asks what time I'm coming home. He usually considers my absence from home a blessing, which gives him time to blast his hip-hop, listen to hot so-and-so on the radio, and stay on the phone until it leaves an indentation on his right ear. But I'd said scarcely ten words to him over the past forty-eight hours.

"I'm leaving right now, Jamal," I said guiltily as I saved my file and turned off my computer.

"Want me to start dinner?" The boy really had missed me, but I sure didn't feel like his cooking tonight.

"No. That's okay, baby. Are you up for a pizza? I'll get one on the way home."

"Sounds good to me!"

I hung up the phone, settled back in my chair, and said a silent prayer of thanks for the life I did have. That I didn't feel like I had to lie about anything in my past or, for the most part, my present. I was lucky as hell.

I glanced at the tape recorder with Pauline Reese's tape, thought about listening to it again, then realized that there was nothing on it I didn't know by heart. I could still hear the inflection of every word she had said. I turned off my computer and got ready to gather my things and leave like I'd promised Jamal I would. I remembered then that I hadn't called my service since Thursday night. In her usual nasal tone, Karen answered on the first ring.

"Well, Ms. Hayle, haven't heard from you in a couple of days.

Everything okay at home? Did you get that flu that's been going around? How's your son doing? Meet any interesting people lately?"

"I'm fine, Karen, thank you," I said coolly, hoping to discourage any further questions. For somebody who has never met me face-to-face, Karen is always in my business and thinks nothing of putting in her two cents worth when I'd rather not hear it. She doesn't mean any harm, and every now and then her observations are helpful, but this afternoon her "concern" was scraping my nerves. I'd had enough intrusion into my personal space for one week.

"Did I get any calls?"

"Just two."

"Who?"

"Both from the same person. Well, they came in last Friday. The person who called sounded like she had something important to say. Said she'd call you later on. Figured you'd talked to her by now."

I rolled my eyes, thankful she couldn't see me.

"Who called me, Karen, and when did they call?" I asked as patiently as I could.

"*Hmmm.*" I could hear her rustling through some papers. I was one of many people whose phone she answered, and she never missed a chance, subtly or otherwise, to let me know it.

"Let me see now. Call came in last Friday. Lady called twice. After seven, which is why I guess you weren't there, huh? I'm glad to see you're taking more time off, Ms. Hayle. You are one hardworking sister lady, and I truly admire that about you, but everybody needs—"

"Who called, Karen?" She snapped to attention at the no-nonsense tone of my voice.

"Pauline Reese."

I couldn't speak for a moment. She must have heard the dead quiet on the other end of the line, and her voice grew grave and serious. "Ms. Hayle, are you okay?"

"What did she say, Karen?" My voice cracked. Karen knows voices like some folks know books, and she understands what the pauses that come between words can mean. She read my voice now, and hers was gentle but efficient when she spoke.

"The first call, she just said she'd call you back on Monday, and then she called back a little later on and she was laughing, like self-conscious. I wrote that down too, Ms. Hayle, like maybe she was embarrassed about bothering you or found something funny and then she said that she'd seen something or somebody. I couldn't make out 'cause to tell the truth it sounded like the lady had had one or two, if you know what I mean. Something or somebody, it sounded like she said, that she thought you should know about, and that maybe it was nothing but that it struck her as strange and it might be important. Then she hung up the phone."

"She said 'something or somebody'?"

"I'm sorry, Ms. Hayle, I wish I'd heard the woman better. I'm sorry. But you know how old Mr. Corn will get to messing with your mouth when he takes you for a spin. You okay with that, Ms. Hayle?"

I told her I was and hung up quickly.

Could I have saved her life?

Pauline Reese had known the person who killed her, I was sure of that. It was somebody who had easy access to both her and the offices. What had she wanted to tell me? Why hadn't I pushed her more about Rufus Greene? I chastised myself again, thought about playing the tape, to hear again how quickly she had answered when I'd brought his name up, but then decided maybe I had imagined it, and that hearing her voice again would only make me feel worse. Pauline Reese was dead. I had missed my chance.

I turned on my computer again, cursing its slowness as I waited impatiently. When it came on, I studied the names in the NN file, reread the notes that followed, then typed in new words—*Deceased, Murderer unknown*—after Tyrone Mason's and Pauline Reese's names. Funny how I had followed his name with hers, as if, like the murderer, following some strange, unpredictable pattern. I stared at her name on the screen, ashamed now of the words. *A bitch on wheels,* I had typed that first time. Her name was followed by KENTON DANIELS III, TANIQUA, MANDY MAGIC, and finally RUFUS GREENE. *If you call it by its name . . .* My grandmother's words came back to me, and I cut them off. I didn't want to hear any of her wisdom tucked away in the back of my mind.

The phone rang, and I turned away from my computer to answer it.

"Jamal," I said, not sure for a moment it was he and then recognized the booming hip-hop. "Turn it down," I yelled from reflex.

"Hey, Ma, chill." He used that patronizing voice that only teenage boys use on their mother.

"I'll be home in a half an hour."

"That's not why I'm calling. Take your time. Take your time. Listen, this . . . uh . . . girl came over to talk to you. Says she knows you and has to see you right away about something." He said the word "girl" with that touch of admiration and interest that men have when they see something they like. I wasn't used to hearing it in his newly changed voice.

"What girl?" I sat up straight, mother's instinct breaking out.

"Hey . . . uh, Miss, what'd you say your name was?" My ears perked up at the flirting tease of his voice, something else I wasn't used to hearing.

"Taniqua," she said.

CHAPTER SEVEN

THEY WERE LOUNGING LAZILY IN MY TIRED OLD KITCHEN chairs the way teenagers do, arms crossed, facing each other. Taniqua's back was to me, but I could see Jamal's face when I came through the front door. He glanced up at me as if I'd interrupted some absorbing confidential conversation. I'd been seeing a lot of that teenage know-it-all sullenness lately. It crops up whenever he feels I've crossed some line I'm not supposed to cross. Usually I ignore it.

My son has become more guarded these days. I try not to take it personally. I know that most of it is simply son-to-mother, male-to-female foolishness, as he stumbles and occasionally trips into manhood. I understand that it comes with the territory. With each inch he grows and each decibel his voice lowers, a new line is silently drawn and a new barrier quietly erected. He is more secretive than he used to be, but he is also more protective. He has a new gentleness too, as if he understands that he is stronger and bigger than I am, and that new advantage brings a certain responsibility. As I walked into the room to confront them, I thought about Jake with an odd mix of anger, gratitude, and regret. Through the years, he has played an irreplaceable role in helping me raise this boy by myself. Jamal had long ago cut his father from his life, and Jake Richards, in his wise and sensitive manner, had filled in so much—and so many times I took him for granted. I wondered how he would react to the situation confronting me tonight.

"Hey, Ma." Jamal quickly rose and kissed me on the cheek the way he always does. "Taniqua?" he smiled flirtatiously, questioning if he'd said her name right. She smiled back and nodded that he had. I didn't smile. "Taniqua said she had something to talk—"

"Taniqua, how are you this evening?" I coolly interrupted him, letting him know by the tone of my voice that I was displeased, letting her know that she had entered a space where she wasn't supposed to be. Jamal's face fell, and he threw me a slightly confused look. She turned around completely to face me, her eyes puzzled, her dark-red lips pouting in surprise. I could see the kid, scared and unsure. I felt like a bully.

It had started to rain when I'd left the office. My coat was soaked, and a line of water had followed me into the room. Jamal pulled some paper towels from the holder near the sink to mop it up, trying to get on my good side. I snatched a towel from his hand and wiped my briefcase, scowling all the while.

"I'd like to see you for a moment, son." I nodded toward the living room. He threw me a doubtful look.

"Want me to get this up first?"

"No."

"Sure?"

"Excuse us, Taniqua." I moved quickly out of the room, followed by Jamal, his head dropped down like a naughty puppy's.

"Whassup, Ma?" he said when we were out of earshot. I snatched his arm and pulled him toward me.

"I'll tell you what's up. Boy, have you lost your mind, letting strangers into—"

"Whoa! Boy!?" he cut me off like a man would, much louder than he should have, which made me madder than I already was.

"Yes, *boy!* As long as you're standing here in *my* house, eating *my* food, listening to a CD player bought with *my* money, you're boy to me," I said, my voice rising an octave, but I noted how tall he towered over me. The men in my family have always been tall, and he fit the mold. I haven't had to reach high shelves, tote groceries, or shovel snow in three years. But sometimes his height and weight work against me, particularly when I yell at him, which is seldom. He has always been a good kid, but I was reminded again as I looked up at him that there was very little I could do to him physically if he chose to ignore me. Luckily, my power as a parent never rested with brute strength or the power of my hands. I've always reasoned with him, and our relationship has always been built on mutual respect as well as love. There was a scowl on his face now, but it broke into a slow smile, and he lowered his voice as he spoke.

"Ma, I'm not a kid anymore." It was information quietly and reasonably stated, not flung in my face. He was turning into the kind of man I'd reared him to be, one who would never raise his voice or hand to a woman.

"I know, son." I softened my voice now, too. "But I don't like you to have strangers in the house."

"But, Ma. It's a girl," he said patiently as if I hadn't noticed and it would make a difference.

"I'm aware of that."

"She rang the bell, we got to talking—"

"About what?" I asked suspiciously, and he paused for a moment.

"As a matter of fact, we started talking about Stan, the cat down the street."

"Stan the cat?"

"He came up on the porch. I gave him some of those cat treats you bought for him, and Taniqua just said she'd always wanted a pet and her mother would never let her have one. Then she started talking about her mother—and how come you didn't tell me you were working for Mandy Magic! How could you not tell me something like that?" An indignant scowl spread across his face.

"Professional discretion. In other words, it was none of your business."

"So we started talking about our parents. She said her moms is really something else. She was talking kind of bad about her. I didn't say anything bad about you, though."

"Thanks for that."

"And it started to rain—hard—so I asked her if she wanted to come in and she said yeah, and that was that. What do you think she was going to do? Drag me into the living room and have her way with me?"

"Now is not the time for sarcasm, Jamal."

"I just want you to give me some credit. I can take care of myself." He pulled himself up to his full height. "What should I have done, just let her stand out there on the porch until you got home?"

"Well, you shouldn't have let her in."

"When she said who her mother was, I knew she was an important client. I didn't want to blow it for you, by letting her daughter stand out in the cold rain. Was that Mandy Magic who has been doing all that calling?"

"Yeah," I said, understanding a little more and not as angry as before.

"And besides that, Taniqua is one fly honey!"

"And that's my point," I said, annoyed again. "She's a pretty girl, dressed . . . provocatively . . . and that was the real reason you let her into to our home, wasn't it?"

He rolled his eyes. "I wouldn't call jeans and a sweater provocative."

"And as I've told you, son, a pretty wrapping doesn't mean doodley-squat if there's a bomb in the package." He stood back, arms crossed at his chest, intrigue beaming instantly in his eyes. If I'd hoped to discourage him, I'd definitely chosen the wrong words.

"So, you're saying there's a bomb in that particular package?"

"All I'm saying is things—and people, for that matter—aren't always what they seem." He looked doubtful.

"Aren't you always telling me not to judge people too quickly, on their background or what they look like?"

"Yeah."

"So?"

"So, what?"

"Maybe you shouldn't judge Taniqua. Maybe you're making assumptions about her." He gave me a triumphant grin.

"Trust me on this one."

"Okay," he said with a furtive glance toward the kitchen. "So can I least say good-bye?"

"I'd rather you didn't."

"So you're going to say good-bye for me?"

"I'll say you had somewhere to go."

"Right." He looked at me critically. "Well, just tell her I'll call her later on tonight," he said with a mocking wink. "After my mommy goes to sleep," he added in an exaggerated falsetto voice. I threw him a dirty look, and he bounded up to his room, two stairs at a time, singing to himself.

When I went back into the kitchen, she had changed positions and was now sitting where Jamal had been. Her eyes were closed, as if she were trying to sleep or forgetting something that frightened her. I tried to imagine her mother's face as I looked at hers. Theresa had not been that much older than she was now. Just turned eighteen. Not that much older than Jamal, not that much older than Mandy Magic when she had become a hooker. A black Coach tote bag sat on the floor beside her. She was dressed like a teenage boy's fantasy—tight jeans, tighter sweater, too much chunky gold jewelry. But even the garish earrings, which hung precariously from the lobes of her delicate ears, didn't take away from her beauty. I could easily see how Jamal—and men twice his age—could be taken with her. *Sneaky* and *sly* had been the words Pauline Reese had used to describe her, but she looked neither now. Just tired and very young.

"Taniqua?" I said her name, as I sat down across from her. She jumped, startled, as if I had awakened her from a nap. "Were you asleep?"

"No. What happened to Jamal?" She opened her eyes lazily and looked around the kitchen. Her voice was surprisingly sultry for someone so young. She looked for a moment as if she if she didn't quite realize where she was.

"He had to go somewhere. He said to tell you good-bye," I said, true to my word.

"He's so nice."

"Does your mother know where you are?" I asked, quickly discouraging any further discussion about my son.

"No. She's had a lot on her, with Pauline's death and everything. I didn't want to bother her."

"What brings you here, Taniqua?"

"I'm scared, Tamara."

"Why are you afraid?"

"Kenton." I tried to read what was in her eyes, and as I did Pauline Reese's brutal assessment of the girl came back to mind.

But how sly could an eighteen-year-old kid be?

"Why are you afraid of him?"

"I think he killed Pauline."

There was no emotion in her voice when she said it, and she didn't look like someone who was afraid for her life. No trembling lips or bugging eyes. Just very calm and cool. *What did she really want?* I wondered.

"Why do you think he killed her?"

"Because he told the police a lie."

"What was the lie?"

"That we were together that night."

"Then you weren't?"

"We were, but then he left." She stood up and then went to the door of the kitchen and looked around. "How big is your house?"

"Big enough," I said, puzzled by her change of direction.

"Just you and Jamal live here?"

"Yes."

"Where is his daddy?"

"We're divorced."

"Is he close to his daddy?"

"Are you close to yours?" I asked, wanting to bring it back to her and why she had come. She cocked her head to the side, as if she didn't quite hear me or didn't understand what I wanted, and then eased back into the chair, her body tense and expectant, her eyes wide. "Why don't you tell me about your father and why you lied to me before about him."

"Rufus?"

"Yeah."

"He looks out for me. He's not like a real daddy. But he looks out for me."

"Does he frighten you?" I studied her for any trace of fear, but there was none.

"No."

"Is your mother . . . is Mandy afraid of him?" Despite what Mandy had said, I was still sure that he had something to do with all this, that he was more involved than either of them wanted me to know.

"Rufus?" she said his name again, mumbling it this time, and a glimmer of something I couldn't identify was in her eyes. But she switched back again, back to Kenton.

"I think he killed her because he said he was going back to the office, to the gym there, and it was late, and he hated Pauline, and he said she should have died instead of Tyrone, and now she is dead, and I'm scared, Tamara." The words came pouring out, like lies might, but there was fear in her eyes now and in her voice. I wondered just how good an actress the girl could be.

"Have you seen him since the murder?"

"No. He won't come out of his apartment. He finally let me in, after I begged him to. I had to beg him though. When I call, he won't call me back, or if he picks up the phone, he'll ask real quick who it is and what I want. He acts like he's guilty of something, or maybe even scared of something, but he won't say what."

"Have you told Mandy about any of this?"

"No. I told you before. My mom is so sad about Pauline, I don't want to worry her. She hasn't been sleeping much."

"Are you afraid that Kenton will . . . uh . . . hurt you too?" I couldn't bring myself to say kill.

"I don't know."

"Why haven't you told the police? They have talked to you several times, right?"

"No. Just once."

"Would you like me to call them make an appointment for you— maybe go down with you so you could tell them what you've told me?"

"No. I don't want to get him in trouble," she said amazingly, but maybe it was herself she didn't want to get in trouble. Maybe she was more involved than she wanted to say. Maybe it was Kenton who should be afraid.

"Have you ever slept with Kenton Daniels?" I took all judgment out of my voice and kept in mind that Mandy Magic had taught the girl to lie well. But her eyes were so big, and she shook her head with such youthful disdain and disgust, I knew she was probably telling the truth.

"Go to bed with Kenton? No. I'm a virgin," she said with a strange mixture of pride and embarrassment that made me smile. And I realized then that there actually was no real reason to assume that they had slept together. Mandy Magic had told me as much during our talk at her house, about his flitting but never landing. I had made assumptions based on the girl from the way she looked and the way she and Kenton had acted together, as if they shared some secret. But maybe Jamal was right about me. Maybe I was judging too quickly and assuming too much.

"Has he ever tried to seduce you?"

"Kick it to me? Kenton? No."

"You seem very close to him."

"Kenton gets me through things sometimes. I help him through a lot of stuff, too. Like Tyrone did." She dropped her head when she said his name, and when she looked up at me again her eyes were filled with tears.

"You really cared about him, didn't you? About Tyrone."

"Like I love my mom and Rufus sometimes. I love him too, kind of sometimes," she added, as if telling me something about Rufus she thought I should know.

"Sometimes," I repeated her word. "And when you say your mom you mean Mandy?"

"My mom," she said it again, firmly with a question in her eyes, as if she wondered why I would think it could be anyone else, and I thought again that maybe she wasn't that sly little liar that Pauline had made her out to be. She began to cry softly then, and I let her cry for a while before I spoke again.

"Taniqua, last Tuesday when I came by your house, you had been somewhere with Rufus . . . with your father. Could you tell me about that?"

She glanced up at me. "How did you know?"

"I just knew."

"To my real mother's grave."

"Do you think about her much?" I realized after I'd said it what a stupid question it was; the look on the girl's face told me as much.

"Late at night I think about her. I think about how we used to talk and about how much she loved me and the things she used to do for me, like giving me her coat when it was cold, like the food she used to make, the soup we used to mix with water to make it go a long way and add hot sauce and some onions, and she would call it Ma's homemade, and it would be *so* good. I cry sometimes when I think about that, and then I think about William Raye."

"The man who killed her?"

"The man I had to kill."

It was the way she had said those words that sent a chill through me, and I thought about that first kill and how no other kill mattered after that. What nightmares had the anniversary of her mother's death and that first kill brought back to her? She closed her eyes again, tightly this time, and she was rocking back and forth in a slow and deliberate rhythm, rocking herself to sleep.

"What's wrong, Taniqua?"

"Everything is coming apart."

"Like that time before?" I took a chance and asked it because I know myself how trauma repeats itself with each anniversary, how violent death evokes the memory of other violent deaths. I knew it because I have lived it myself.

"Why does everyone I love always die?" She asked it like a little girl would, a sob riding the edge of her words that shook me to my soul. I reached across the table and took her hand. That was mother's instinct too, I guess, as strong as it had been in protecting Jamal. But she stiffened, as if catching herself, and I knew she was wary of me. Instinctively, I drew back, and she dropped the hand I had held into her lap, balling it into a tight little fist.

"Sometimes when horrible things happen close together like this it seems like that is all there is, that there will be no end to it, but that's not the way it is," I said. "Things will be different for you . . . and for Mandy. I promise you that."

"You can't really promise me that, can you?"

"No, I can't."

"Do you know yet who killed Tyrone?" The tone in her voice was baiting, almost antagonistic, daring me to say something concrete, and I knew I couldn't.

"No."

"But you promised that too."

"No. I never promised anyone that."

"But you haven't found out anything yet, like you said you would."

"No, I haven't. But maybe you can help me with something."

"What?"

"I need some more information."

"From who?"

"Maybe from you, Taniqua. I've heard all kinds of things about Tyrone, from all kinds of people. Why don't you tell me about him?" She pulled in her breath through her nose and settled back into her chair, and after a moment she spoke in a voice so low I could barely hear her.

"He could be nice. He showed me what to wear and how to do my hair. He told me secrets. Other people's secrets." She smiled mischievously, and I smiled, too, as if I understood. "But I could get mad at him. I'm mad at him now."

Was this what I was looking for?

"What did he do?"

"Because of something he had in the album he left me. The pictures I found. They were bad pictures of my mom. They made me mad." She reached into the bag that rested at her feet and took out a bunch of photos held together by a rubber band. I knew then why she had come.

There were six of them, all dull and distorted with age and bent as if they had been tucked away and forgotten. As I glanced through them, the look of the clothes they wore—the bell-bottoms, halter tops, and platform shoes—told me they had all been taken around the same time, late sixties and early seventies. All were of Mandy Magic. Starmanda Jackson.

The first two were obviously of her when she had been on the block. She wore a teenager's daring, fuck-you smirk, her long hair flipped up on her head in a tacky upsweep, her makeup was heavily applied. She was dressed to sell, her hot pants and halter leaving no doubt as to what she was selling. And she was dressed all in red.

Red for that Chanel suit. Red for that ruby she wore on her fingers. *Red for Rufus Greene.*

He leaned against a red car in this photo. Age had not been kind to him, I realized. He had once been handsome, in that hardened, inaccessible way some women find appealing. His skin had been clearer back then, and he had been leaner, but his eyes still stared in that invasive, penetrating way. The last two photos were different from the rest. I turned them over; there was no date or writing. Both were of Mandy, holding a tiny baby wrapped in white blankets. The man who stood beside her looked like the photograph of Tyrone Mason I'd seen and was obviously Harold Mason, his father. I assumed the baby was Tyrone. This was not the Mandy of the other photos. She seemed more fragile, sadder, her shoulders dropped low as if in defeat. Her dull blue dress might have belonged to somebody else; it hung loosely off her small frame. In both pictures, she turned her face slightly to the side, perhaps trying to avoid the camera, and her eyes were cast down. Her face was clean of makeup, even lipstick. She was very different from the tough little mama who had been in the first two photographs.

"So that was Harold Mason," I said quietly.

"He must have loved Tyrone. He looks so happy," Taniqua said.

"You've looked at these pictures a lot, haven't you?"

"But I don't want to see them anymore. Except for my mom and Rufus, everybody in the picture is dead. Except for my mom and Rufus."

I went through them a second time, then handed them back to Taniqua.

"I don't want them." She put them face down on the table as if they had burned her hands.

"You came to show these to me, didn't you?"

"Yeah."

"Did you know about your mother's—both of your mothers'—and your father's pasts before you saw them?"

"I figured it out."

I sighed as I took the photos up and went through them again and then fastened them together again with the rubber band.

"Mandy and your mother were very young," I said as gently as I could. "Younger than you even. They made mistakes as we all do. When you get grown, you look at your mistakes. You know they are part of you, so you give them their due, and you understand that as awful as they might be, they have made you stronger. You've lived through them, and that is all that counts." I tried to pull out what little wisdom I had about such things. She said nothing, her eyes too sad for someone so young.

"So Tyrone had these put away?" He had probably found them by chance in his father's albums when he died, the same way Taniqua had found them in his. But they had given Tyrone Mason a ticket to the good life, at Mandy Magic's expense. Twenty grand to keep this secret, to keep the photographs to himself. Tyrone, more than likely, had recognized himself and his father in that photograph and been able to place it in time. "Who else knows about the photos?"

"Rufus. He was in one. He said he remembered when they were taken."

"Does he know that you're showing them to me?" If he had been involved with Tyrone somehow, in blackmailing Mandy, I might be in more trouble than I knew. She glanced at the window, and my eyes followed hers. "He brought you here?" Dread swept through me, and I searched her face for the answer and some hidden message or agenda because her eyes shifted away from mine. But she was just a scared kid, I decided. There probably was nothing more to it than that. "I'll drive you home. Don't bother to call him back," I said quickly, trying to take the alarm out of my voice, making it sound as casual as I could. But I knew I was vulnerable, and I was afraid.

CHAPTER EIGHT

I HAD GOOD REASON TO BE AFRAID. HIS CAR WAS SITTING outside my house when I came home from work the next night. I came inside quickly, slammed and then locked the door behind me and checked on my son, who was in his room doing his homework. I dreaded looking out the window, so I waited half an hour before I checked again. He was still there, waiting outside my house like he had been at Mandy Magic's last week. I don't like being afraid. I don't like the way the pit of my stomach tightens or the coldness that comes into my fingertips. I don't like the sound of my heart pounding in my ears.

Jamal seemed oblivious to my fear, which was surprising because he usually reads me like a book, but he was preoccupied this evening, and I was thankful for that. I didn't want my son, with his newly emerging sense of machismo, to feel it was his duty to protect me. Fortunately, he had a chemistry test the next day and alternated bites of Crock-Potted chicken with glances at his notes during dinner. It was his night to clean the kitchen, but I excused him so he could study. He gratefully dashed upstairs and closed the door behind him, and I heard the blast of his CD player after a while, which he claimed he couldn't study without. I didn't go upstairs for our usual heated discussion about it. I just let him be.

I cleaned the kitchen slowly, paying particular attention to a grape-juice stain that had worked its way into my more or less white Formica countertop two weeks ago. I even spent ten minutes polishing the copper bottoms of one of the Revere pots I'd inherited from Johnny. Anything to waste time before I glanced out that window again. It was going on nine when I finally did, and his car was still there. I put on my coat and went outside to confront him. I could see him watching me in his side mirror as I approached.

"So you finally got your pretty ass out here," Rufus Greene said, as he climbed out of his car and leaned against it in what he obviously thought of as striking a cool pose. He was dressed in green sharkskin this time but without the wide-brimmed black hat. His hair was thinning on the top and sides. His teeth, which were small and uneven like those of a child, broke the menace of his pockmarked face when he spoke.

"Why are you parked in front of my house?"

"I want to talk to you."

"About what?"

"Something that needs to be said."

"Get the hell away from me and my home before I call the police."

"You going to call them dogs on me? For what? I ain't done nothing to you. I ain't even parked in front of your damned house. I'm 'cross from it. You gonna get the police after me for doing nothing." His eyes narrowed with outrage. I'd seen that anger before—in the eyes of criminals who had had more than their share of run-ins with the law. But I'd also seen it in the eyes of innocent black men roughed up by cops for no good reason. I'd seen it in my son's eyes.

"Why are you here?" I realized that calling the cops was not going to be an option.

"I told you that. We got to talk."

A narrow band of light flickered in my neighbor's window, which told me that she had pulled her shades to the side to check out what was going on. I cursed silently. That woman minds more of my business than I do. All I needed was for her to start telling folks that I was keeping hours with a former pimp. With an old hustler's nose for sniffing other people's discomfort, Rufus Greene glanced around my neighborhood. A sly grin eased itself onto his face.

"You got a nice place here, Tamara Hayle. I can tell you growed up nice around here, ain't never had to face the shitload of problems a lot of the rest of us had to face. Even my own daughter had to face. Taniqua." He studied me for a reaction when he said her name. I held my face tight. "You want to hear what I got to say about her, don't you? I ain't going to say it standing out here in the cold."

"You're certainly not coming into my house." I toughened my voice and my stance. He reared back, reassessing me and the situation.

"Ain't nobody said he want to go into your house."

"Then I guess we stand out here."

"I ain't got nothing to say to you then." He turned to leave.

"It is about Taniqua?" I wasn't ready to let him go.

"Yeah, Taniqua and the other one."

"Theresa?" Surprise and then sadness sparked for a moment in his eyes. "No. Starry."

"Mandy Magic?"

"Yeah. Starry." The bravado was back, along with the cockiness. "Who else you think it's going to be about?" He looked across the street at my house and at the other houses in my block. "I want you to hear it because I respect you, Tamara Hayle. I respect you."

"You don't know me."

"I don't never go nowhere without knowing where I'm going. Come on." He nodded toward his car. "I know you don't want me in your house, and I know you won't come to mine. Let's go somewhere we can talk, public place, but we can talk private. I'll tell you what's on my mind." He paused for a moment before he added, "I trust you 'cause my daughter do. You can trust me for that reason too." His voice was strangely seductive, and with uncomfortable insight I knew what had once drawn weak, very young women to him. It was that sinister mixture of need and raw power that filtered through in his voice and manner, all tossed together with an undertone of pure, dark sexuality. But it held no magic for me.

"I'll follow you in my car," I said.

"Suit yourself." He climbed back into his car and gunned the engine, letting it run. I went back into my house and told Jamal that I had to go out and I'd be back. I also went to my closet and pulled out my .38, which had seen more action in the last two days than it had in three years, strapped it into my shoulder holster, and got ready to follow Rufus Greene.

The gun was heavy, not like the lighter ones some folks carry these days, and I felt a strain in my back and neck when I sat down in the Blue Demon. But it wasn't the weight that made me uncomfortable; it was the possibility of having to use it. With a man like this, though, I knew I'd best have it; that possibility could easily become a reality.

But who was a man like this? I watched his shadowy outline as he bopped to the beat that was obviously blasting from his car's CD player. At nineteen he had been a pimp. At twenty he'd been run out of his hometown because he wasn't as tough as he had to be. He'd fathered a child with a woman who had been his whore. I had no sixth sense about him, no way to judge or second-guess him. I had street smarts, I was sure of that, but this man had lived through more than I had ever experi-

enced. He had come of age in a world of which the only thing I knew
I'd gotten from B movies and old TV shows.

But he was a parent, and I understood that. He loved his child. He
had supported her, tried to play some small part in her life, which was,
as I thought about it with annoyance, more than I could say my ex-
husband, DeWayne Curtis, had done for my son in the last year. And
there had been that change in his manner, as slight and barely percep-
tible as it had been, that had come when I mentioned Theresa.

We drove into a part of the city that I'd never seen before, a side
street off a deserted one that looked like it hadn't been repaved since the
1930s. There was a dreariness to it, a deadness that made me fearful of
what I would find. He slowed down on a narrow street where children
played in an abandoned car and an elderly man, sitting in a broken
kitchen chair, talked to himself as if he had been forsaken by the world.
The despair on his face made me think for a moment about Johns, the
man from the parking garage, and then of my father and how little of his
life had been good. Except for us. Maybe Taniqua was all Rufus Greene
could pull out from the spoils of his life, too.

He parked in front of what looked like a storefront bar or club
with no name. The window had been painted black, and the building
next door had been gutted. He got out of his car and walked toward me
with a nod for me to follow. I hesitated a moment, wondering if maybe
I should turn around and head back to the parts of the city that I knew:
downtown with its sparkling new arts center and newly awakened hope.
The Ironbound, with its restaurants sweet with the smells of lobster and
saffron rice. The Central Ward fish-fry joints and incense-scented mom-
and-pop stores. But this was a part of the city that knew no hope, rougher
even than the projects where I grew up.

But the bar didn't look too bad inside. It was dim, with secondhand
plastic-backed chairs and a couch that took up most of the room. A bar
upholstered in red-and-black tweed was tucked into a corner, and an ancient jukebox, which could probably bring a nice piece of change in an

antique store, sat in the corner. A man in his late sixties sat on a stool behind the bar, his face transfixed by the light of the TV in front of him. The place smelled of cigarettes and hard times, but the liquor bottles that stood in a gleaming line across the back wall were premium, the brands drunk by men who like it straight. It was the kind of place that my father hung out in when I'd been a kid, more a social club than anything else, the type frequented by aging hustlers with nothing to show for their lives but old scars and stories nobody wanted to hear.

But there was nobody here to listen tonight. Rufus Greene was surprisingly polite as he showed me to a corner table. I sat facing the door, Wild Bill Hickok–style, not wanting any surprises. The bartender brought him a bottle of Courvoisier and two glasses. He nodded to ask if I wanted one and poured himself some, swallowed it in a long, loud gulp, and then quickly poured himself another. I thought about Pauline Reese.

"Why have you brought me here?"

"I needed you to know where I come from. Where we all come from. My roots and all."

"I've seen them. What do you want to say to me?"

"Hey, hold on a minute, baby. I ain't too old to forget what it's like to sit across from a pretty woman."

"Drop the shit and get to the point." I cut my eyes at him to let him know I wasn't playing around. He took another swallow, slowly and with obvious pleasure, letting me know that I wasn't going to rush him and that I was on his time.

"I don't trust a lot of people—you should feel complimented," he said, and I shifted uncomfortably in my chair. He smiled. "Taniqua says you got a boy, around the same age as her. Says he's a nice kid. Says she liked talking to him. I saw him when he come home from school. Look like he might play some ball or something like that. Looks like a good boy. I thought you'd understand what I'm going to tell you. You got a kid the same as me."

I wasn't sure what he meant by all this, by mentioning my son like he had, but I didn't like it. I stared hard at him, at the way his face was suddenly empty of feeling and how he lifted his head, checking me out like he didn't give a damn about anything in the world. I studied the homely face and the eyes that could pierce your soul, as they now looked into mine. My heart beat fast. I didn't let the expression on my face betray my fear.

"Don't ever mention my kid again," I said so low he had to lean near to hear me. "Don't mention his name or where you saw him or anything about him. Do you get that?" He studied me, as an amused grin came to his lips. I didn't blink or breathe. His eyes softened, and I remembered what Mandy had said about him, how she had been tougher than he was. And I was tougher than Mandy.

"Okay," he said, which I knew he would because he wanted something that only I could give him, whatever it was.

"Now tell me what you want."

"I'm scared about my daughter," he said it softly. Maybe it was the words said as they were, or the same urgency in his voice and sorrow in his eyes that made me think about Jake, who was as different from this man as any two men could be, but the devotion and worry they both felt came from the same corner of their hearts. "She's involved in something. I don't understand it. I don't know what it is. All I know is I don't want to lose her like I did her mama. When I'm just getting to know her good. Be with her good."

"First tell me about Mandy Magic." He looked surprised for a moment, and then his body stiffened as if it was settling into something that made him uncomfortable. Then he relaxed and grinned, taking his time again.

"She still wearin' all that red?"

"Yeah."

"She look good in it, don't she? She didn't think a dark-skinned gal would look good in red till I told her. Ain't nothing prettier against skin as dark as hers then red. Shows it off, all that pretty black skin. She ain't forgot that, has she? She ain't forgot what she come from."

"What did she come from?" I asked, even though I knew.

"Poor as snot, like the rest of us. Trying to make something out of nothing."

"Like the rest of you?" I asked like I didn't know, and his eyes left mine for a moment, as he said the names softly to himself that Mandy herself had mentioned.

"Me. Bunny, Jewel. Ruby—that was Terrie's cousin. All of them. Starry was what I called Starmanda. That's her real name, Starmanda Jackson. I don't know where she got that Mandy Magic shit from, but Starmanda Jackson was the name her mama gave her, the name I knowed her by."

"When did she start calling herself Mandy?"

He tapped his fingers on the side of his glass, as if he were thinking of something, and then glanced up at me, a puzzled expression on his face. "She didn't tell you much about herself, did she?"

"No." He laughed a rough guffaw that filled the empty room. The man watching the TV glanced up at us with annoyance and then back at the set.

"She ain't changed too much then. She never did tell nobody much about herself."

"So she made the name up?"

"Naw. EB gave her that name, Mandy. Sound like a white girl, don't it? But he liked his ladies like Starry. All black and pretty like that."

It took me a moment to realize who EB had to be: Elmer H. Brewster. The rich white man who Pauline had said owned the station where Mandy worked and that she eventually bought. The place where her life had begun to change, where Starmanda Jackson had become Mandy Magic.

"And you introduced them, EB and Starry?"

He chuckled salaciously, telling me without saying anything the nature of that introduction.

"How old was she then?"

"EB liked them young. Unspoiled. But wasn't too much *that* girl hadn't done or been done to her. She tell you about Mason? That son of a bitch who got her when she was a kid."

"Yes."

"She told you about that, huh?" he chuckled and then stared at his drink as if he were talking to it. "I stomped his punk ass down his throat when she started working for me. Can't tolerate no man like that having his way with a young girl. I was nineteen and I knowed that shit. Stomped his punk ass right straight to kingdom come. Favor to her. Birthday present." He said nothing else about it, but I began to realize where some of her loyalty to him may have come from. He took another drink as if recalling with some pleasure his actions. "She just turned fifteen when she started with me. I guess she was close to sixteen when I introduced her to EB. Young and pretty and black. And once she started with him, he didn't want her with nobody else, so she didn't go. Not to my knowledge anyway."

"How old was he?"

"Early seventies maybe. Hard to tell with old white men."

"And he knew she was that young." I tried to remove the judgmental tone in my voice; it didn't work.

He shook his head as if amazed by my naïveté. "Where you been, baby? Where you grow up? In a garden? The only way an old man like that can get it up half the time is to fuck something that's tits stand high as his dick droops. But Starry had something else going for her that EB liked. She was smart. Starry always been smart. EB was smart too, and they just naturally hit it off because of that. He was good to her too. Got her back in school. Gave her one of them jobs at his station. Made sure she didn't have to do nothing she didn't want to do to make a living. Paid me to look out for her, half the time, keep her off the street. A real live sugar daddy. Young whore's fantasy. Ever see that movie *Pretty Woman*? I saw that thing and I said to myself, ain't that just like Starry and EB, 'cept EB didn't look like no Richard Gere."

An angel disguised as a devil.

"Did EB leave her everything when he died?"

"No. He just made it easier for her to survive. Told her how she could do it. Drilled it into her. I used to tell EB he treated her like a daughter. Guess he liked fucking his daughter." He laughed and then shook his head as if he didn't understand it. "Starry was in her late twenties when he kicked, and by then she was 'Mandy Magic' with a new name, her own show, and everything else." He paused for a minute as if thinking of something that hurt him, and then he shook his head in wonder. "Had to get it from a white man, though. That's the thing I hate about black women. Always getting something from a white man. That's a damn shame, ain't it!" He polished off the liquor in his glass in a long gulp and poured himself another, glaring at me.

"Is that what you hate about her? Because she pulled herself up with the help of a white man? Is that why you and Tyrone Mason blackmailed her about her past and why you wrote her those two notes to scare her after you killed him?" It was a long leap, but I took it anyway, wondering as I said it if this whole thing could have originated from some distorted take on black male pride.

He looked at me curiously. "You think I hate Starry? I don't hate that woman. I don't hate her 'cause she don't forget nothing. Nothing. That's why she took my daughter in like she did. Tyrone Mason? That's the little faggot that got his throat cut, ain't it? I don't have no beef with Tyrone Mason. He was nice to my daughter, so I don't have no beef with him. You better ask his boy Kenton Daniels the Third about that action."

Only the tops of his small teeth showed when he smiled, but the snide, nasty way he'd said it told me what he meant.

"They were friends?" I asked as if I actually had grown up in a garden.

"What do you think, baby, two men like that, acting like they acted to one another."

"But how that could be? I thought maybe Kenton and Taniqua were in some kind of a relationship?"

"Taniqua is too young to be having anything with anyone," he said indignantly, like a protective father would, which surprised me.

"How well do you know your daughter?" He looked lost for a moment, and then a shadow came over his eyes, veiling the levity that had been there a moment before. He smiled again but not like before, and there was a tenderness and a pride that I was used to seeing in Jake's eyes when he talked about Denice.

"She's a tough little something. Tougher than her mama, tougher than me even, but I wonder sometimes what it will take to break her." He glanced up at me, his head cocked to the side as he continued. "I can look at your face and tell you don't think much of me, do you?"

"I don't like pimps." I told it like it was.

"I ain't a pimp no more. That shit went with my hair." He made a pass at humor; it missed its mark.

"I was a boy myself, and I've forgiven myself for what I was. Me and God, that's the only ones who got a hand in it, Tamara Hayle. I wasn't there for her mother, but I'll be there for her. She's all I got left of myself, the only thing decent I got to show for my life. I'll die to protect what is mine. If I had been there for them, she never would have had to kill that man like she did. Protecting herself and her mama. That was my job, not hers."

He stood up as if inspired by his own words and walked over to the jukebox. He put in some money, watched it for a while, and then came back to where we sat, listening and nodding his head to himself as an old Smokey Robinson tune played. He seemed lost in his own thoughts for a while as I was lost in mine.

"How did she kill him?" I asked finally, because I knew somehow that whatever he wanted to tell me had to do with the man that his

131

daughter had killed, and with the memory of her mother and what he hadn't done and should have.

"Do you know what it is to kill a man?"

"Yes," I said, because I did.

"To feel that blade, to twist it, feel his flesh move 'neath your hand like bread. To see the blood splashing out him like nothing you ever seen in your life. You stab a man to death, you getting down to his essence, ain't like shooting somebody. There ain't no distance between you, no bullet taking his life. It's just you doing it. Like strangling somebody or smothering them. You can feel the life ebb out of him, and there ain't nothing like that in this world."

He glanced up at me, taking in the horror that I knew was in my eyes. But I could see the same horror in his. He glanced away from me then, in what looked like shame, and continued, "That's what my baby did—stabbed William Raye in his heart and watched his life run out of him on the floor where she was standing."

And once you've tasted blood, had that first kill, nothing means anything anymore.

"So this was what you needed to tell me? That Taniqua has killed a man. That she watched someone she killed die?"

"That's part of what you need to know. What the girl has seen. What she has been through. What she did."

"How much of what she has seen is part of her now?"

He didn't answer me but said instead: "You got a big heart, Tamara Hayle. I can see that in you. My daughter knew it—that's why she come to talk to you. Will you protect her from what's after her? Will you promise me that? I ain't got nothing to give you 'cept the fact that I'll owe you, and I'm a man who pays his debts."

"But what am I protecting her from?"

"I don't know," he said, his eyes as desperate as any man's I'd ever seen.

CHAPTER NINE

I DIDN'T LIKE RUFUS GREENE, AND I CERTAINLY DIDN'T trust him, yet I couldn't forget the anguish that had been in his eyes when he'd begged me to protect his daughter. But when I told Mandy Magic about our conversation the next morning, she showed no concern or emotion. I should have known her reaction would be as calm as it was. I had to see her in person to get to the truth. Her face was what always gave her away: the droop in her eyes, the hesitation when she chose her words, the sardonic curl of her lip. Her beautiful voice was how she made her money, and she controlled it well.

I knew how devastated she had been by Pauline's death, yet when I listened to "The Magic Hours" at night, it was as if nothing out of the ordinary had happened. She was her old self when she got on the radio: self-confident, helpful, as wise as she'd always been to the helpless and hapless. She buried that needy, frightened part of herself—the shaken Mandy whom I had seen more often than I wanted to in the past few days—and became Ms. Mandy Magic, her voice as clear and true as it always was. "Welcome to 'The Magic Hours,'" she'd say each night, with no hint of the troubles she'd seen. Some folks might say she was just good at her job, a bona fide professional talk-radio host, who could put her personal woes behind her. But I sensed it was something more, that there was some fundamental piece of herself that was missing, something she'd erased in order to survive.

But she wouldn't be able to hide from what was to come. Weeks later, when I'd put enough space between myself and what happened to breathe a few good breaths, I wondered if there was anything either of us could have done to change things. Hindsight, though, is always twenty-twenty, and when I called on Kenton Daniels that Thursday afternoon, I had no sense that things could turn so violent as quickly as they did.

A visit with him did seem to be the next logical step for me to take. Both Taniqua and Rufus Greene had hinted that Kenton's relationship with Tyrone Mason was more carnal than he wanted folks to know, and if that was the case, I knew he probably had a hand in blackmailing Mandy. I didn't yet understand her relationship with him, even if Kenton "swung both ways," as they sometimes put it. I didn't know if I could trust Taniqua's take on his involvement in Pauline's murder, but I did know that the police had their suspicions about him too, which was enough for me. The brother was hiding something. I could feel it in my bones.

Yet I didn't feel he posed any *real* threat to me, which could have been foolish on my part or just plain whistling in the dark. But he did know the police had their eyes on him, and the last thing he needed was a murdered PI showing up somewhere in his vicinity. Truth was, when it came to Kenton Daniels, I was less concerned about him than about how I'd break the news to Mandy that a man she'd kept so close was possibly part of Tyrone's blackmail scheme. So I again packed my tape recorder in my bag as I slipped my gun into my holster. Call it insurance.

I called Kenton Daniels from a pay phone across from his building. There was no answer at first. I remembered that Taniqua had said he'd been avoiding answering the phone, so I waited five minutes, tried again, and let it ring for a while before I hung up. An answering machine picked up on the first ring, which told me he'd probably just switched it on and was sitting by the phone anxiously monitoring his calls. In my best professional voice, I identified myself and explained that I had some information about Pauline Reese and Tyrone Mason that I was ready to share with the police, but out of courtesy to my client Mandy Magic, I'd decided to share it with him first. I added that my "sources" had informed me that he had *not* been where he told the police he'd been the night of Pauline's murder. I also mentioned that I was in his neighborhood and would call back in five minutes, and if he still wasn't home, he could contact me at my office later and take his chances about reaching me. As I assumed he would, he picked up before I hung up good. He spoke in a careful, halting voice, as if he hadn't quite made up his mind what to say—gone was the cocky Kenton Daniels III who had strutted around Mandy Magic's house like he paid the banknote. He finally agreed to see me but made me promise I would come alone and vowed he wouldn't let me in unless he was sure of it.

His apartment building had been built in the 1920s and showed its age. It was located just shy of the border of Belvington Heights and Bloomington, where Wyvetta said Tyrone Mason had once lived, close enough to the Heights to have cachet, but definitely on the low-rent side. His old-fashioned elevator had an "Out of Order" sign thrown sloppily across its door. I was glad his apartment was on the second floor. As I walked through the deserted hallway and up the poorly lit stairs, the ceiling lights flickered so badly I was afraid the whole place would be plunged into darkness. Needless to say, I didn't waste any time getting to where I was going. Luckily, I'd turned on the tape recorder in the hall. Kenton opened the door before I had a chance to knock. No doubt, he'd been staring out the peephole waiting for me.

He was dressed in red sweat pants and a filthy white T-shirt, and his face and neck were damp, as if he'd just showered. His sneakers were untied, and he looked like he needed a shave. The apartment smelled musty. His place was a hip, funkier version of Mandy Magic's living room—flowery chintz thrown together with kente cloth, dainty glass statuettes mixed up with Zairian masks. English country meets citified Africana. The shades were pulled down blocking the sun, which made the place seem smaller and darker than it was; it could have been midnight as easily as noon. A torn gym bag, made of some strange metallic fabric, sat on the floor beside him. The words "Gandy's Gym" were printed in peeling gold across it, which hinted that he had just recently come back. An ancient set of dumbbells of varied sizes and weights rested in stands in a far corner of the room, and they looked weapon-ready if he was so inclined. I was glad I'd strapped on my gun. I sat down on his small mud-cloth-draped couch and placed my bag on the table. He dragged over a chair from the dining room and settled down across from me, his left foot patting the floor in an unsteady rhythm. Forgetting the small talk, I got right to the point.

"Did you kill Pauline Reese?" His mouth dropped open, he bugged his eyes, and he reared back his head dramatically.

"Who do you think you are coming in here and asking me some bullshit question like that, like a goddamn cop? I got to hand it to you lady—you got some serious balls on you. *Cojones*, isn't that what they call them? Who told you something like that?"

"Let's try Taniqua." I trotted her name out to get a reaction. He gave me what I was looking for.

"Taniqua." He repeated her name with a delicate, affected air. "Why would she tell you something like that?"

"Because she is afraid of you."

"Taniqua, afraid of me? Taniqua is my girl. I don't believe it." He dragged the towel across his face and neck, then leaned back in his chair, his face still puzzled. "Did Mandy tell you that?"

"I haven't mentioned it to Mandy." He went back to toweling off his neck, lightly patting his shoulders, which was obviously something to do to avoid looking at me.

"Why not? You're working for her, aren't you?"

"She has a lot on her mind, and I didn't feel like burdening her with the fact that her boyfriend might have killed her best friend."

"I'm not her boyfriend. Mandy doesn't have a boyfriend or man-friend or girlfriend or any kind of friend that I can think of, now that Pauline Reese is dead. I think Miss Mandy has seen enough sex for one lifetime."

That little quip told me he was definitely aware of what Tyrone Mason had on her, but I didn't let my face show anything I knew. But I did pop the Tyrone question: "So what kind of a relationship did you have with Tyrone Mason?"

"You didn't come up here to talk about Tyrone, did you?"

"I think it's all connected," I said truthfully, probably giving away more than I should have.

"You said you knew something I should know," he said, eyeing me suspiciously. "You said you knew something about Pauline's death."

"Tell me about Tyrone first."

He glanced away, his face grew grim, and his shoulders suddenly drooped, as if someone had reached inside him and pulled him into himself. I decided to throw it all out.

"Were you lovers?"

"No." He gave a what-the-hell shrug and added, "Not yet, any-way."

"You wanted to be, then."

"I hadn't come out yet, admitting to the world that I was gay." He walked to the refrigerator and opened it noisily. A rush of stale air tinged with the smell of spoiled food and rotting vegetables floated into the room. He pulled out a small bottle of Evian mineral water, opened it, and poured the water into an elegant long-stemmed water glass, and he sat back down across from me, crossing his legs.

"You ever know what it is to be between and betwixt, not knowing where you fall, who or what you belong to? Probably not." He studied me for a moment and then added with a contemptuous chuckle, "You strike me as the kind of lady who always knows exactly what she is, where she comes from, where she is going." I gave a half-smile, struck by how much he'd gotten it wrong. But the mood in the room had changed. It was lighter, more relaxed. For the moment, anyway, he seemed at ease with me.

"Appearances can be deceiving."

"Yes, they are." He pulled his chair closer, adding a sense of confidentiality. "They never knew what I was when I was a kid," he said after a minute. "You probably didn't know either when I first walked into Mandy's office. People have been wondering about me all my damn life. Is he black? Is he white? Is he Latino? Is he East Indian? Half the time I used to lie about it because I didn't know myself."

"They gave you a hard time about having light skin?" I asked the obvious.

"White boy. That was my nickname, white boy. Until finally I got sick of it and swore I was going to be as tough as the blackest Negro I could find. So I ran with the baddest crew there was in high school. I had the money and they had the cool, and they didn't mind a 'white boy' if he could pay his own way and theirs too. Finally my mother, rest her sweet, unenlightened soul, sent me to a rich kid's prep school in Boston. They thought I was Puerto Rican up there, so I became Spic, and that was sure closer to what I was than white boy, so I figured I could live with that. Too white to be black, too black to be white. It's a bitch, ain't it?"

"Kids can be very cruel." I mouthed the conventional cliché.

"My father was a saint, though, wasn't he?" A tight smile crossed his lips. "Black and proud, even though his skin was as yellow as mine. He definitely knew who and what he was, and he never let anything take that away from him. His father, my grandfather, was like that too. Ever try living up to a legend?"

I smiled sympathetically because I did know what that was like. My early days on the police force had been an exercise in being as good a cop as I thought my brother had been, constantly trying to live up to his legend, his good name, until he'd blown his legacy away along with the top of his head. But that had happened a long time ago. I could remember now without pain how hard I'd worked to serve his memory. Kenton gave a burst of short, light laughter when he read the look of understanding that had come into my eyes.

"You know what I'm talking about, don't you?"

"I know."

"But as it ended up, light skin was the least of it. When I was up in that school in Boston. I had, well, this experience." He paused for a moment playing with the towel, wiping it around his hands, avoiding my eyes again, and then he folded it, placed it on his lap as if he'd made some kind of decision. He looked at me straight without blinking or shifting his gaze. "I fell in love with another man. It didn't last because I couldn't face my feelings yet, and I've regretted it ever since." He waited for a reaction that I didn't give.

"And Tyrone Mason was the second man you fell in love with?" I jumped ahead of him, anxious to bring Tyrone into it, but he didn't let me rush him.

"I didn't so much love Tyrone as admire him. He was openly—proudly—gay, and he would spit in anyone's face who didn't give him his due."

"I've also heard some other things about Tyrone, not quite so flattering." Kenton shook his head in agreement.

"Tyrone was the kind of man my mother would have called a

scoundrel. He was disgraceful, but he knew who he was, at least in terms of his sex thing, and that taught me something about myself. We weren't lovers, but he helped me understand that there was nothing wrong with being who I am, what I am. He took me into a world where I belonged, and I'll be thankful to him for that for the rest of my life."

"Did you know he was blackmailing Mandy Magic?"

"I figured as much. She is a keeper of secrets. I left it alone. I have my issues with Mandy, too."

His attitude toward the blackmailing of his friend—and benefactress—bothered me, and I pushed it further. "Did you write those notes?" He looked genuinely offended.

"No. I assumed the person who was working with Tyrone wrote them. And get this straight. I didn't have anything to do with Tyrone blackmailing Mandy. I never even knew for sure." He walked over to the other side of the room to pick up one of the smaller barbells and flexed his arm several times, holding it tightly. I was relieved when he put it down.

"Who do you think killed him?"

He sighed and shook his head. "I honestly don't know. Tyrone took a lot of chances. He liked picking up trade in that park. He liked the thrill of it. It could have been one of those guys. Maybe the cops got it right for once." He sat back down, dropped his head into his hands for a moment or two, and then continued. "He was really okay. I know that this all makes him sound like a bastard, but he was really okay. He was nice to Taniqua. Real nice. I kind of try to fill in for him now. But I'm not Tyrone. I don't have the kind of patience with her he had. He told her about me." He looked worried for a moment, and then his face relaxed. "He told her about me, that I was trying to come to terms with myself and all that. At first I was mad about it. I figured it was my secret to tell, but she's never told anyone about it."

"And you're sure about that?"

He looked worried for a moment and then shrugged. "It doesn't matter one way or the other now."

"So what do you think about Rufus Greene?"

"I try not to think about Rufus Greene."

"Then you know who he is."

"Taniqua told me."

"Have you ever talked to her about her relationship with her father?"

"No," he said too quickly, and I figured that like most folks, Kenton Daniels was just telling those parts of the truth that would do him the least harm. I couldn't entirely blame him for that. But I still hadn't gotten the full story of his relationship with Mandy Magic. Despite what Pauline Reese had told me, I wondered if it had been Tyrone Mason who had orchestrated their first meeting, so that they could scheme on Mandy together. When I asked him, though, his explanation verified what Pauline had told me.

"She introduced herself to me at some society something or other." He took a sip of Evian, sipping slowly from the glass as if it were champagne. "She said she knew my father," he added after a minute. "I was standing there with this girl I'd been going out with. I was still trying to get it on with girls at that point. Mandy came up and asked if I was related to Dr. Kenton Daniels, Jr., and when I told her that I was, she gave me her card and said if there was anything I ever needed to give her a call. I couldn't believe it. Neither could the girl for that matter."

He smiled as he recalled the meeting, shaking his head in amazement. "So the next morning, before she forgot about me or got sober or something, I gave the lady a call. I thought at first she was trying to pick me up. A lot of older ladies tried to do that with me, you know," he smiled coyly, as if he were proud of it. I nodded my head enthusiastically, with what he probably took for understanding. "Mandy was on the level, though. I was just about broke at that point. She hired me as a consultant and interior decorator and just generally looked out for me."

"Wasn't that kind of strange, just to take you in like that?"

"Yeah. It struck me as strange too. But she can do that sometimes, be generous and kind for no apparent reason at all. Then she can turn on you like a viper or a pit bull. Bite you twice before she says good morning."

"You said earlier that you had your issues with her."

"We all did, all of us. Me. Pauline, Tyrone, even Taniqua in her teenage, angst-ridden way. We're dependent upon her for everything. Basically we're nothing without her." He said it as if it was a common fact, as if it didn't bother him or embarrass him to be in that position and to admit it with so little shame.

"But that's not Mandy's fault."

"That depends on how you look at it. She never gives you what you're worth. Sometimes she can be a royal pain in the ass, although when you first meet her you think she's got it altogether." I didn't say it, of course, but I understood only too well what he meant.

"Did she ever say what her connection to your father was?"

"Just that she owed him a favor, that's all."

He smiled slightly and then added something as if he had just re-membered it. "When she first met me she said she'd seen a photograph of me on his desk in his office. I must have been a kid then, because she said I was in a garden. It was my mother's garden. I couldn't believe she'd actually remember something like that. She must have been a kid herself."

"So you met Tyrone after you started working for Mandy?"

"We used to kid about it. She hired Tyrone because she was close to Daddy Harold, as Tyrone used to call his father, and she hired me be-cause my old man had done her some favor. Funny thing was, neither of our fathers could stand us."

He studied me for a moment, wondering, I assumed, whether he could trust me, his eyes distant as if he were having some kind of argu-ment with himself, and they seemed to darken with worry or suspicion.

142

"You got the time?"

"It's going on four."

His foot started to tap the floor again, drawing my eyes to it because it was the only sound in the room. He got up suddenly, glancing around the room as if he were going to straighten it up, as if he were expecting someone. Things had changed, and I wondered why. "You've been here too long. I got to get ready to go."

"Are you afraid of something?" I didn't think he was going to answer me for a moment, but he finally did.

"Yeah. The person who killed Pauline Reese." He said it lightly, so I didn't know whether to take him seriously. He glanced at the door, self-consciously, then back at me. "You said when I let you in here that you had something on the person who killed her. Did they send you? Since you haven't shot me yet, I assume they want something. What is it?"

I paused before I answered him, not sure what to make of him, where to take it next. His eyes begged for some truth I didn't have and never did.

"Tell me what you know first," I said.

"I told you the truth."

"About the night Pauline Reese was killed."

He shook his head in denial, without saying anything for a moment, and I answered for him. "I know you weren't with Taniqua like you told the cops. Where were you?"

"Don't you know?"

"You were there, weren't you?" I took a chance, playing a hand I didn't have. As luck would have it, the tape recorder in my bag began to make a strange popping noise. We both glanced at my bag in the same moment.

"What's in the bag?" His eyes narrowed with suspicion. I had no choice but to play it straight.

"I sometimes use a tape recorder in my work." I pulled it out, took out the tape, and handed it to him. "Here. You can have it. I'm sorry."

"Bitch," he said between his teeth.

"Not bitch, just careful." The atmosphere in the room had quickly changed to one of distrust and animosity.

"Who sent you?"

"I'm working for Mandy Magic," I said weakly, and he ignored me.

"What do they want?"

"Who?"

"The people who sent you." His voice had taken on a paranoid tone that sounded comical, almost ludicrous.

I paused. "If you were there, then you must know what they want?" I decided to play it his way.

He stood and walked away from me and then turned back around to confront me, which was startling. His face was distorted in anger, and I stood now, too, ready to protect myself if I needed to, wondering how long it would take to get my gun if I needed it.

"Why are you playing games with me?" He spoke in such a hushed voice I could barely hear him. I gave a furtive glance toward the barbells in the corner of the room. Other than his hands, they were the only weapons he could use against me. I wondered how far he would go, and how violent he could become if pushed. But I was sure he'd noticed the bulge under my jacket. His face broke suddenly, and his bottom lip began to tremble. "What do you want from me?"

I had the upper hand now, I was sure of that, so I bluffed him as I tried to see what he knew. "If you were there, then you must know who it was."

"What did they say?"

"Nothing." I played it by ear.

"Why did they kill her. Why? I hated her too. But why kill her?"

"If you were there, and if you saw who killed her, why haven't you gone to the police?" He scrutinized me and then thrust out his chin, suddenly insolent.

"Don't think I won't. You can tell them that too."

"Who is *them?*" I asked in a quiet voice, trying now to recover the bond we'd had before he'd discovered the tape recorder yet knowing that his momentary trust had been lost forever. He shook his head, as if trying to empty it of uncomfortable thoughts, figure things out, and as I watched I had the fleeting thought that maybe I should have played it straight. "You don't know, do you? You were there and you didn't see who it was, did you?"

"No."

"And you're afraid that I'm here with some message from the person who killed her, aren't you?"

"Stop fucking with me! Stop jerking me around!"

"I'm trying to find out what happened, so I can help you."

"Nobody can help me." The terror in his eyes told me that he was afraid of me, and I didn't like that feeling.

"I'll be straight with you now," I said finally. "We can stop playing games. Nobody has sent me. I don't know anything more than you do. I always tape sensitive interviews. Sometimes it's with the person's permission. Sometimes it's not. I don't like doing it, but it comes with the territory.

"Taniqua came over to my house night before last and said that she thought you killed Pauline Reese. She said you weren't with her like the cops think, that you'd gone off by yourself. Why don't you tell me what you know? Everything that happened that night."

"What did Taniqua tell you?"

"That you were with her that night, but that you left an hour or so before Pauline was murdered."

"Okay," he said as if he were tired of hiding things. His eyes didn't leave mine as he told the rest of it.

"I never knew much about Taniqua's history. Tyrone knew, but he never told me. Do you know what it is?" I nodded that I did, and he paused briefly and then continued. "She told me for the first time that night. I don't know why. She said things were all coming back, how she had stabbed that guy to death and how it was really jerking her around because Tyrone had been stabbed to death, and she was all messed up about it, and she didn't know what to think. Things were too close, she kept saying.

"I didn't know what she meant, but then the whole way she was talking made me uncomfortable. She's just a kid but with a history like that . . . after Tyrone's death and everything . . . I just didn't want to be around her. Bad vibes, I guess, call it whatever you want to, but I've been pretty messed up myself lately. Maybe I was wrong, but I didn't want to be around her. Her killing a man like that and all. She gave me the creeps."

"So you dropped her off at Mandy's that night?"

"No. She didn't want to go home. I dropped her off at this place where she meets her father sometimes, this hole in the wall in Newark somewhere. She went in to wait for him, and I went home. I got home and still felt restless, and working out helps me when I feel that way, so I figured I'd walk over to Gandy's and get the extra exercise, but by the time I walked over there, the place was closed, and I didn't feel like walking back, so I hailed a cab. When I got in the cab with the gym bag and everything, I figured I may as well go to the gym in the office, get a cab back, so that's what I did." He stood up, as restless suddenly as he'd said he'd been that night, as he paced once around the small room and then sat back down. I watched, saying nothing.

"So Rufus was with her the night Pauline died?"

"I don't know. I just dropped the girl off at that hole in the wall and then came back." He looked lost, as if he didn't know what else to say or as if he would be uncomfortable saying it.

"Take it step by step," I said, trying to coax him, but he looked through me as if he hadn't heard.

"I got to the office, unlocked the office door, and glanced into Pauline's office. She looked up when I came in but she didn't say anything, just threw me one of her nasty looks and went back to work. I cursed the woman out under my breath, like I always did, and went into the gym. It was at the far end of the hall, down from her office. She could be a class-A bitch, and that always pissed me off, her not even acknowledging my presence. I slammed the door and locked it, figuring if she came to say something to me, she could go to hell.

"I punched the bag for a while, did some weights, then the Stairmaster. I heard the front office door open and close and figured she was leaving, so I didn't pay it any mind. Then about fifteen minutes later, I heard it open and slam shut again. I stopped working for a moment, listened, heard her go into her office, and figured she'd forgotten something. Then I heard it slam closed again about ten minutes later. I figured she'd left again.

"I got on the treadmill, which is noisy as hell because it's cheap, put some James Brown on my cassette player, and started running. I heard a crash and a bang, and it must have been loud because I heard it through JB. I snapped the cassette player off to listen. When I didn't hear anything, I yelled out her name, and then I heard somebody come up the hall to this office and try the gym door. I was so scared I almost peed on myself, and I was damned glad it was locked. I asked who was it, but by then whoever it was had left, that damn front door opened and slammed again, hard." His eyes darted first to my face and then to his door and then back to my eyes, holding them fast.

"I called out to see if Pauline was all right, and then I waited for about ten more minutes, picked up a dumbbell to protect myself, unlocked my office door, and went to her office to check. Her door was open, and there she was, with that cord wrapped around her neck like a noose. I don't even remember leaving the room or getting my bag or even leaving the building. But I remember the cold hitting me when I got outside. I remember feeling like I was going to vomit, trying to keep it in, so I wouldn't do it on the street like some ignorant drunk or something. It's strange the kind of dumb shit that comes to your mind when something like that happens. I went to a phone booth down from there and called the cops. I couldn't stop shaking because I knew that whoever it was had come back for me too."

His foot was tapping again. A door somewhere down the hall slammed shut. He jumped at the sound, his eyes big with fear.

"I know they'll come back for me, because they don't know if I can or can't identify him or her. They don't know what I heard or didn't hear. They don't know if I saw them or not."

"They know you haven't gone to the cops yet."

"But they don't know if I will."

"Then you have no choice but to go."

"The cops will think I did it," he said forlornly. "They've questioned me twice. They know how she hated me, how I hated her. If they can place me there that night, they'll think that I killed her. I know they will. Then they might even pin Tyrone's murder on me. I don't have an alibi for that night, either. They'll assume we were lovers the way you did, and they'll think I killed him and then her. There's something else you should know," he added after a moment, leaning toward me and speaking in a low voice as though there was somebody else in the room. "Tyrone gave me some of that money, that ten grand he got from Mandy. It was a loan. I was going to pay it back. I think Pauline may have known about it. I'm sure she did."

He'd obviously forgotten that ten minutes ago he'd hinted he hadn't definitely known about the blackmail. My suspicion about him kicked in. *Had I read him wrong?* I wondered. *Was he lying about the rest of it too?*

"So you did kill her, didn't you?" I said like I was finally on to something, which I wasn't. But my voice was cool, and I kept my eyes pinned to his, waiting for them to drop; they didn't. They were completely blank. I wasn't sure about him, how truthful he had been, if he was really as scared as he seemed. I sat up straight, ready to go for the gun if I needed it. He looked surprised and then angry and apprehensive, like he realized he'd made a mistake.

"Oh, God," he said.

"Let me run it down to you *another* way." I watched him for any small reaction, but he seemed too surprised and shocked to protest. "You knew she was there that night, working late. You parked your car at home. You went there in a cab. You let yourself in. You argued with the woman. She confronted you, probably about the money that you and Tyrone blackmailed Mandy to get. Maybe she hinted that you had something to do with his murder, taunting you about your relationship with him. You got mad. You didn't mean to lose it, but you grabbed that phone cord and killed her, wrapping it around her neck and pulling it as tight as you could. And you didn't call the cops, you let her lie there like some dead bird until somebody found her and called the cops. You're telling me all this to see how it goes over, to see if I really have anything on you.

"But I want to set you straight about something. If something happens to me, you'll be right in jail where you belong because a lot of people know I'm here, and I expect to walk out of here the same way I came in. So why don't you just come clean with it, stop hiding from the world, and get it off your chest."

"Fuck you," he said in a small, scared voice. "I told you because I thought I could trust you."

"Let's call the police, and tell them what you know," I said more gently.

"No way. I'm just going to keep my mouth shut and get the hell out of here as soon as I can. If I tell the cops, they'll arrest me for her murder. They'll connect me to the game Tyrone was running on Mandy the same way you did, and they'll say I killed her to keep her quiet, the same way you did."

"What's to stop me from telling them what you've just told me?"

"It will just be your word against mine. And I know that Mandy will cover for me with the cops when I say I dropped Taniqua off with Rufus, because they might suspect her. Taniqua didn't like Pauline either, and the cops know that because I told them. Nothing is more precious to Mandy than Taniqua," he said it with a touch of envy that surprised me.

"And where was Taniqua and her low-life daddy when Pauline got offed? Maybe Pauline had something on the two of them too." He spoke conspiratorially, as if we were on the same side, comrades in arms fighting the same battle. But he wasn't saying anything that hadn't crossed my mind. He changed directions then. "They know who I am, but I don't know who they are. I'll be okay as long as they catch who did it, whoever the hell it was. But until they have, I'm going to make my-self scarce, like I said."

"What are you going to do?" I asked with some concern.

"Never mind."

"Your best bet is the police. Get yourself a good attorney, tell him what you know, and then go to the cops. I'll go with you if you want me to."

"I don't trust you anymore," he said petulantly, like a spoiled child.

"I'm sorry. But I had my doubts, too."

"Forget it," he said lightly like he meant it, with a devil-may-care shrug. "Will you please go now."

"Listen to me, Kenton. Go to the police with me now. I have a gun, so nobody will hurt you. The cops can offer you protection if you tell them everything you know, starting from the beginning, no lies, no trying to fool anybody."

"No."

"Are you sure? Maybe you—" He cut me off.

"Will you please go now," he said again, his voice polite with the good home training that his "sweet, unenlightened" mama had probably taught him, but his eyes—like those of some small hunted animal— darted toward the window and around the room. So after shaking his hand and wishing him luck, I left. And that was the last time I saw him alive.

CHAPTER TEN

HIS KILLER HAD WAITED FOR HIM IN THE SHADOW OF THE stairs with a knife sharp and swift enough to take his life quickly. Kenton Daniels was killed not at night but early in the evening, only hours after I'd left him. Except for his killer, I had probably been the last person to see him alive, and his tense words to me may have been the last he spoke to anyone.

Had I led his killer to him?

He or she would kill again, I was sure of that, moving on up until Mandy Magic would become the final victim. But could the danger lie closer than she thought?

I was on my way home from work the next day when the report of his death came over the radio. I had nothing in particular on my mind; my thoughts were running randomly, from the sad state of the Blue

Demon to whether I should stop by Dino's Pizzeria for that pizza I'd promised Jamal two days ago. I nearly lost control of my car when I heard the report. Swerving into the right lane, I turned quickly, my tires squealing as I barely missed another car. I couldn't think or feel for a moment. Somehow I managed to get to the curb, drawing in my breath as deeply as I could, then letting it out slowly, thinking even as I did that I was drawing breath that he would never take again. I closed my eyes, still numb from it, prayed for a moment, and then just sat there, thinking about what I had just heard.

Movin' on up.

Tyrone Mason. Pauline Reese. Kenton Daniels III. They had been murdered according to their closeness to Mandy Magic. *Tyrone Mason,* the son of Harold, whom she had loved. *Pauline Reese,* her dearest friend from the Starmanda Jackson days. *Kenton Daniels,* another son of a dead man, another tie to her past. And who was left? *Taniqua.* And what did that mean?

I thought about Rufus Greene then and his terrible words about killing a man, describing it as if he had held the knife himself. I thought about Taniqua, closed my eyes, squeezed them tight, trying to erase the memory of his words from my mind, thinking instead of Kenton Daniels III and what had been taken from him.

I had been there. I had seen him. Now he was dead. Had his killer been watching us, hidden in some dark corner, waiting for me to leave or for him to sneak out on some insignificant errand—a carry-out from a restaurant, a quick workout at the gym, fast money from the ATM to get out of town—and then killed him for what he or she thought Kenton knew?

I assumed that Mandy Magic had heard about it by now, that the cops had filled her in on this latest killing of someone close to her. I was certain now that they would listen to what I had to say and take it seriously this time. There were too many coincidences, two deaths in less than six days. But I knew I had to speak to Mandy Magic before I discussed her case with the police. I owed her that much, both personally and professionally.

And I would have to tell her my fears about Taniqua. They were vague and unconnected, sixth-sense more than anything else, but they were real, and I couldn't shake them. I was sure the girl was involved in some way, although I had no idea why or how deeply. And I knew another thing: This danger was stronger now, closer to Mandy, and more eager to strike her down than it had been before.

Movin' on up.

Was that danger Taniqua? Had that first murder triggered something within her?

You ever get the feeling that something horrible is right around the corner waiting to get you, some big old nasty something that will turn your life to dirt? . . .

Something was waiting for her, yet I knew she would be afraid to even say it, unless I somehow forced it out of her.

Who was the silent one, the deadly player, in this?

Pauline had been killed before she could tell me. Kenton Daniels was killed because someone thought he knew. And Mandy had to know something more than she was telling. Death was striking too fast, too often for her not to know, if only she would let herself admit, even to herself, what it was.

I stopped by a drugstore and called home to tell Jamal I'd be home late and to remind him to lock the door and not let in any strangers — no matter how well he thought he knew them. He knew whom I was talking about, and the seriousness of my voice told him I wasn't playing around. I called Mandy Magic's house next, and when she didn't answer, I hung up quickly and drove to her house to see if she was all right, not letting myself think about anything except getting there.

She answered the door on the first ring, her scarlet chenille robe drawn tightly around her thin frame. Red-and-black slippers were on her feet. Her pretty face was drawn, and her eyes were swollen. She spoke in a monotone, her face placid. Except for her eyes, it was impossible to read her.

"I couldn't take anything else, any more bad news," she said when I asked her why she hadn't answered the phone. "I can't believe he's gone."

They had called her late last night, she said, after they had discovered and identified his body. Her telephone number had been underlined on a sheet of paper on his desk, so they assumed she must be a significant person in his life. Although she wasn't his next of kin—there was no next of kin as far as anybody knew—the police had done her the courtesy of telling her the news before they gave it to the press. She was Mandy Magic, after all, and that name deserved and demanded respect. She had been dealing with the pain of it ever since.

We sat down in her Laura Ashley living room, with its green and pink chintz. The silver cigarette case lay open and empty, and the stale smell of old tobacco filled the room. The carved ebony box where the two pistols lay sat where it had been before. There were no remnants of a dying fire tonight, and the room was strangely cool. I shivered when I entered it; perhaps it was my imagination.

I sat beside her on the couch, and Taniqua settled across from us, where Kenton had sat when I'd been here last. Her eyes were swollen too. Her long hair was pulled high on top of her head with a rubber band, and she looked more like a little girl than anytime I'd ever seen her. She barely spoke. I tried hard not to look at her.

There were still signs of Kenton's presence in the room: a *Sports Illustrated* lay open on the table, a pair of men's black house shoes were pushed under the chair. I thought again about what he had told me about his and Mandy's relationship and about the one he'd had and not had with Tyrone. I knew I should question her about it, sensing that perhaps some answers lay in that, but I knew my questions would have to be gentle ones, ones that wouldn't alarm her or disturb the peace she was building within herself. But for now, the three of us sat silently, as if at a vigil. Mandy spoke first, her voice drained of feeling.

"I hadn't really talked to him since Pauline died. I called him, left a message. He wouldn't call me back. The police told me yesterday afternoon that they thought he knew more than he was telling, more than he wanted to admit," she sighed and then glanced at the empty silver cigarette case before her. Taniqua, reading her needs, went into the kitchen and came back with a pack of Newports. I remembered the first time I'd seen her, the self-assurance in her voice when she'd commented about the habit that she seemed so sure she would break. But there was no pretense of breaking it now. She needed every crutch she could get, even though her voice was hoarse and raw from them. She tore open the pack and lined them up carefully in the case. She took one out and quickly lit it, drawing in the smoke hungrily, and blowing it out as if she were releasing every bit of grief she'd felt over the past several days. "He was scared of something," she said after a moment. "I could tell that from his voice."

"He was in your office suite when Pauline Reese was killed." I offered the little bit I knew. There was no sense in keeping his secret now, that need had died with him. But I watched Taniqua's face as I spoke, wondering if I should force from her where she had been that night, she and Rufus Greene. Taniqua lifted her head slightly, as if she had heard something that interested her.

"I was right then," she said after a moment, her voice unnaturally high. "I was right about Kenton and Pauline."

Mandy looked puzzled, glancing at me for explanation. Taniqua obviously hadn't told her yet about her suspicions, and though I had told her about my visit with Rufus Greene, I hadn't mentioned that her daughter's visit had preceded it. I told her now, summing it up as quickly and objectively as I could.

"Taniqua was afraid that Kenton had something to do with Pauline's death." Mandy's eyes widened, and I answered her unspoken question. "They were together that night, as she told you and they told the police that they were, but he left her. He dropped her off with Rufus that night. Then he went to the gym and then to the office to work out there. He was there when Pauline was killed. I'm sure that whoever killed Pauline killed him too."

Her hand flew to her mouth, stifling a gasp, and there was a momentary glimmer of disbelief in her eyes. I thought again about that "big old nasty something" she'd said was looking for her and I wasn't sure about how much of it was sitting in this room with us.

"Could I speak to you alone?" She stared straight ahead not answering. I glanced at Taniqua, silently asking her permission. She looked at me strangely for a moment, as if she knew what I was going to say about her and was wondering if she should leave, and then she got up and left obediently, without glancing at either of us, her back stooped slightly, like an old woman. Mandy watched her go, then got up and cracked the window after she left. Cold air swept in from outside. She closed her eyes to savor the feel of it in her face, taking it in as if it offered her something she didn't have and needed.

"Where was she last night?" I asked her. She closed the window and sat back down.

"What are you getting at?"

"I think you know. Where was she yesterday, when Kenton Daniels was murdered?"

"No!" The word flew out of her mouth, a smack in my face, but I didn't flinch.

"Tell me where, Mandy."

She leaned back, as though daring me to ask something else, and then she answered, her voice calm and defiant. "She was with me."

"Only you know the real answer to that. But at least tell yourself the truth. Was it possible she could have had something to do with Kenton Daniels's murder? He was stabbed, too."

"What do you mean by that?"

"Like William Raye was killed. Like Tyrone Mason."

"She loved Tyrone Mason."

"So she says."

"Those killings don't mean anything. They don't mean a damn thing. What could that mean—the fact that they were stabbed? Nothing. Not shit!" Her voice was breathless, the words flying from her mouth in rapid fire.

"Did she go out yesterday afternoon, maybe to the store, to the mall?"

"I told you, no."

"Was she with Rufus Greene?"

"I told you she was with me."

I looked for some giveaway sign that she was telling me the truth, hoping for her sake that she was but still doubting her.

"I'm going to have to go the police," I said after a moment. "I don't know what happened. I don't know whether Rufus Greene had something to do with Kenton Daniels's death, or if Taniqua did, or what or who is involved, but I don't understand what is happening here. Kenton told me some things—"

"What things?" she interrupted me, her eyes boring into mine, as if sheer will alone could force the truth from me. I stared back at her, not intimidated.

"That he was scared of somebody. That he was upset when he found out Taniqua had killed William Raye. That—"

"William Raye doesn't have a goddamn thing to do with what has happened. He's dead. Theresa is dead. Taniqua is with me in the here and now—"

"Like you always are, right here in the here and now," I interrupted her this time, not minding the mocking tone of my voice or the way I seemed to be taunting her with it. "And now, of course, there really is nobody around who knew you when." I thought for a moment that she was going to slap my face.

"What a stupid, bitchy thing to say," she said, her voice low and hurt. I didn't respond because it *had* been a bitchy thing to say, and I meant it. She'd said her share of bitchy things to me. "What else did he tell you?" She shifted back to Kenton Daniels.

"About the way you two met. That you knew his father. That Dr. Daniels had done some favor for you way back when. What was that favor, Mandy? What favor could a doctor like that, a doctor who ran a clinic for pregnant teenage girls, do for you? Were you pregnant by Elmer Brewster? Abortions were illegal back then, but did you have an illegal abortion—was that what it was?"

Her eyes watered suddenly, and she covered her face, hiding them. I reached over and peeled her hands away, making her confront me with the tears that now ran down her cheeks.

"Tell me the truth, Mandy. Please."

"He was none of that." She sat up straight, pulled in her breath, getting it together with that strength I'd always admired, the one thing about her I knew I'd take with me when I left.

"You're hiding something, Mandy, like you always do." I kept my voice low now, but I didn't conceal my frustration. "You have to tell me the whole truth, whatever it is."

She looked at me for a long time without saying anything and then shook her head, showing that she couldn't or maybe wouldn't break, as if she were shaking off something that she wasn't going to let bother her. I continued talking, searching her eyes for an answer. "Is it something to do with Taniqua and these killings? Or Kenton Daniels? Or maybe Rufus Greene? You know something that you're not able to tell me, something that only you could know?" I was pleading with her, and I don't like to beg. She smiled slightly, looking me straight in the eye yet talking past me, her voice even and defiant, and then I knew she'd won.

"I know that Taniqua is more important to me than I ever thought anyone could be. I can't let anything ever hurt her again. I know whatever you say or do or think will never take that from me. I know that I am in control, not you. I know that I will not be beaten down."

Taniqua came in and sat down on the floor beside her mother's foot. Mandy touched her gently, stroking the soft puff of hair on top of her head as if she were still a little girl. I understood that urge, a mother's need to protect her child. But did this protection run the risk of endangering other people? Taniqua reached up and took her mother's hand, as if holding it for strength, and then let it go. But her eyes darted to the door and then back again, as if she were waiting and looking for someone else in the house. Puzzled, I glanced there too, but saw no one. She returned her gaze to her mother.

"I saw Kenton yesterday afternoon," she said. "Before he was killed, stabbed like that. My mom said not to say anything about it, but I saw him outside his apartment, and then I left."

She had been that last person he seemed to be expecting, the last person to see him alive.

"Did he say anything about meeting anybody else?" That would be too much luck to hope for.

"No."

"What did he say?" She glanced at Mandy, as if asking permission, and Mandy shook her head that she should say no more, but she continued anyway.

"He said that you had fooled him. That you had accused him of killing Pauline. That you weren't to be trusted."

"But *you* accused him of killing Pauline. You told me *he* should not be trusted." I corrected her, trying to keep my voice detached and professional.

"No, I didn't," she said. Anger flashed in Mandy's eyes, and then she glanced toward the hall, where Taniqua had looked. I looked over my shoulder, sensing an unseen presence.

"Is somebody else here, Mandy?"

"No. Just leave me and my daughter alone, keep away from us."

She said the words quietly, but her eyes squinted malevolently, as if merely speaking or looking at me was difficult. I was stunned by her voice, the rage that seemed to come from nowhere, and by the look in her eyes. Taniqua began to cry, and Mandy pulled her close. "Please go," she said, her voice trembling.

I stared at her in disbelief. "After all this?"

"You are fired." She pronounced each word slowly, enunciating in her best radio tone, the words lingering in the air after they had been spoken.

"What?"

"You can't do anything else. You just bring trouble. Go." My astonishment clearly written on my face, I didn't budge. "Leave! Did you hear me? Leave my house!" Her voice was strong now, the taking-care-of-business, Mandy, the in-control magical Mandy of the radio. She was back to her old confident self.

I'd had enough. I couldn't find the words to say what I was feeling, and, in truth, I knew there wasn't a hell of a lot to say. So I stood up and made my last speech to her—collecting my things as I did it, officially withdrawing from her case.

"I'm glad to be out of here," I said, having no trouble at all with the truth. "But you should understand, Ms. Magic, that I'm going to go to the police and tell them what has happened here, what happened yesterday with Kenton Daniels, and everything that you've told me, that Taniqua has just told me. If you feel that this is a betrayal of our contract, then we can settle that later or you can report me to my licensing board or do anything else you want to do, but our association is officially ended as of this moment, as well as any loyalty I may have had to you." I paused, standing now for emphasis, but her face was completely blank as she listened.

"Did you hear me just tell you to go?"

I stood my ground. Determined to say my last words, I continued, "I have an idea who wrote those notes, but I'm not sure why, and I have no proof, and at this point my guesses could do more harm than good, so I won't even bother sharing them—and you didn't pay me for guessing anyway." She looked up at me, her eyes unchanged.

"I didn't solve your case, but I put in nearly two weeks of work, so I will consider your retainer only partial payment for my services. I expect to be compensated for the rest of my time, so expect my bill in the mail."

"Fine," she said, and her voice was empty of everything, not disappointment or even anger. "Close the door tightly on your way out."

"Good luck to you," I said with a dignified nod and what I hoped was the proper amount of professional detachment. *Good goddamn riddance!* I said to myself.

I knew she had fired me because I brought her too close to herself, too close to whatever she was she didn't want to face. But I didn't care anymore. I felt light, almost like laughing at the whole damn scene, as I walked to the door. This case—Mandy Magic, her half-assed way of telling the truth, Rufus Greene, her troubled Taniqua, the whole damn bit—had been more of a strain than I'd allowed myself to acknowledge.

I try not to get too involved with my clients, but I always end up doing it anyway. It comes with the job—caring enough to put myself on the line for them, to risk my life, even sometimes. I like to think that's what makes me a good PI, caring enough about people and their problems to give everything I've got, and I had cared about Mandy Magic. But it was time to stop caring now. So when I closed the door behind me, I closed my life on her too. The cops could take over now.

I walked fast down the walk, past the hedges, my heels tapping hard on the cobblestoned walk. I didn't look back, even though I was tempted to. I heard sounds of partying several houses down from hers. Soft, sophisticated jazz floated out to the street. I could catch a glimpse of shadows as they moved before the shaded windows. I imagined the pops of champagne corks and the clink of good crystal. People having a good time, living it up, enjoying life, which was more than I'd been doing in the last few weeks, thanks to my former employer. Expensive cars—Sevilles, Lexuses, Porsches—had taken up more than their fair share of spaces up and down the street, and I'd had to park the Blue Demon nearly two blocks away. It was probably a good thing. It gave me a chance to mull things over as I walked toward it. I'd been so involved in Mandy Magic's problems, I'd hardly had a chance to pay attention to my own. What I needed was a party. Loud music, fast dancing, good times rolling. My mind lingered for a moment over where my next job was coming from, over the money lost and spent. But I still had some left from the retainer, and I'd just have to think of a way to cut some costs until I got another job.

I'd never been fired from a case before and I didn't like the way it felt. I don't like to fail. I never like starting a job and not finishing it. It always leaves a sour taste in my mouth, and despite my immediate relief at being rid of Mandy and her problems, I could still feel the unpleasant sting of defeat—to say nothing of the possible loss of revenue. My head dropped low for a moment. I forced myself to pick it up.

Keep your head up. Keep your head up. The lyrics from a hip-hop song that Jamal had been blasting for the last few weeks from his CD player rang in my mind, and I smiled, which felt good. *What the hell,* I thought. I'd been through worse than this, and always made it to the other side. I'd make it through again. I tripped over an uneven crack in the sidewalk, and nearly fell. I straightened up, got my balance back, looked around to make sure nobody had seen me, and then laughed out loud, not caring who heard me. I should be thankful for small blessings, I realized. I could have fallen and broken my hip, smashed my nose, cracked my front teeth—but I'd caught myself in time. I always did.

Mandy Magic née Starmanda Jackson aka Starrie had certainly been one of my more interesting clients, and being her confidante for nearly two weeks had been a unique experience—something I could impress my grandchildren with—or even Jamal if I felt like talking about it in the next decade. One thing was for sure: I'd never be able to tune into "The Magic Hours" again with the same feeling.

But I carried some scars too: living through the horror of those two murders; seeing Taniqua cozied up to my son in the kitchen. There had been a lot of things that had saddened me about this case, and Taniqua was the one that touched me most. But that was over now, too.

I glanced at my watch. It was later than I thought, and I sure didn't feel like talking to any cops tonight. I'd go tomorrow morning. First thing on Saturday morning. I thought about Jake then. Ordinarily, he'd be the one who would accompany me on a mission like this—my legal counsel, my "protector" in any uncomfortable legal situation in which I might find myself. But I couldn't call him now. I wouldn't. I'd simply have to get some bucks to pay for legal counsel down the road if I needed it. I'd pretty much decided not to call Jake Richards again until . . . until what, I wondered for a moment. Until he dumped Ramona Covington? Until he owned up to a relationship that he wouldn't admit having? I turned it over in my mind. Should I call him? No. I was still angry at him—but for what? For admitting it? For *not* admitting it?

What was he doing tonight, I wondered. *Was he with her?*

It didn't matter, I told myself. I wouldn't let it matter. I've always had a certain toughness when it comes to men. When it hurts too much to keep it alive, when the pain outweighs the pleasure, and when I finally decide to let it go—it's gone. I didn't yet know if I could change the way I felt about Jake and if it would be possible to love him any other way except the way I did. But if he was involved with Ramona, I wasn't sure if I could take it. When I'd seen him last Friday in my office and told him we were finished, I'd meant it in more ways than I'd wanted to admit then. But what would my life be like without his friendship? He was as close to me as any man I had ever known. How would it feel *not* to have him in my life?

The weight of somebody's hand on my shoulder blocked my

thoughts. He snatched me around to face him, and the scream that was in my throat got stuck there.

"Not so goddamn fast," said Rufus Greene. "You promised me you would protect my daughter, now you talk about going to the police. You ain't going nowhere near no goddamn cops." I could feel the blood rush to my head, the faint music and laughter of the partygoers in the house up the street and a distant horn from somewhere faded as my fear took over. He had been at her house, and he had followed me from there. He had heard me tell her about going to the cops, and that was why he was here.

I yanked my arm away. "Keep your damn hands to yourself."

"You ain't going to no goddamn cops."

"I'll go to whomever I feel like going to, and take your goddamn hands off me." I sounded tougher than I felt. My knees were shaking.

"You ain't going to no cops. Tell me you ain't going to no cops."

I pulled away from him and started walking again, but he put himself in front of me now, blocking me. I tried to go around him, shove him to the side, but he stepped in front of me again. Cat and mouse. A predator and his prey. I didn't like the feeling. And he still had his hands on me, loosely on both my shoulders, as if we were a couple, discussing some private matter. His eyes were desperate with the same desperation I'd seen before, the same apprehension. I knew he was a father protecting his daughter, but I felt no sympathy for him. Yet I managed to put some into my voice when I spoke to him.

"You think she killed him, don't you? You think she stabbed him the same way she stabbed William Raye." I faced him; there was no way around him.

"No," he denied it, but there was no use lying about it. I could see the truth in his eyes. He stood close to me, too damn close. I could smell the cheap hustler's perfume he wore. I thought about the stink of those white flowers on Mandy's Magic's desk that first time I met her, and my stomach turned. From somewhere I pulled up some calm, not letting him know how fearful he made me feel.

"If that's what happened, if you're right about it, then she needs some help."

He looked lost. "Goddamn," he said under his breath. "God-damn."

But he still had his hands on me, and when I tried to pull away, he tightened them. I felt the pressure of his fingers, individual, tiny vises pressing into my shoulders. "Where you going?"

"None of your damn business."

"You ain't going to no cops."

"Did you hear what I said, asshole? Let me go." I pulled away from him, using all my strength, but he was stronger than I thought. Rage boiled up inside me at how he made me feel. I reared back and kicked him as hard as I could in the shins. He looked startled and then dropped his hands and bent down, grabbing his leg.

"Damn you!" I tried to make a run for it but he grabbed me, snatching me around to face him again. I cursed to myself, wondering why I'd let my anger get the better of me. The fool was bigger and stronger than me. I should have played up to him and kept my feet to myself. But it was too late now. I was going to pay for that kick; I could see the fury in the twist of his mouth and in the grit of his tiny teeth.

"Let her go," said a voice from behind me.

"Who the fuck are you?" A look of indignation crossed Rufus Greene's face, as he stared past me at the man.

"I said let the lady go! Let the lady go!" The man repeated the words nervously twice, staccato-like. His voice was vaguely familiar, from some place I couldn't recall. I strained to place it, to remember where I'd heard that voice before. I tried to twist out of Rufus Greene's grasp, turning my head trying to catch a glimpse of the man, but he stood too far to the side.

"I said let the lady go!" The words came out in an angry slur this time, his voice shaking with rage. Rufus Greene dropped his hands to his side, his palms opened, showing he posed no threat. The man shoved me out of the way. He was strong, surprisingly so, and I fell against a car. I felt a sharp pain in my ribs as I hit it, and my arm still hurt from the strength of Rufus Greene's fingers. But I recovered quickly and spun around to face my rescuer. I saw that he had a knife.

Rufus Greene towered above him, and I could see the malice and disbelief in his eyes as he stared down at him. The man lunged toward him quickly, cutting him fast, the way a snake strikes, and a thin line of blood peeked from the slash, cut like a tribal mark on the side of Greene's face. Rufus looked at the man in disbelief, and the man slashed again, cutting his shirt this time, in a slash that left a thin streak straight through to his brown flesh.

"What the fuck!" Rufus yelled, and the man slashed again, as quickly as anything I'd ever seen. I could make out his face now; it was clearly revealed in the dim streetlight. It was Johns, the man from the parking garage. He held the knife up toward Rufus, threatening him again, equalizing the battle.

He looked different tonight, away from the garage and the setting in which I was used to seeing him. He no longer seemed so old or defeated. He stepped forward menacingly. The blood dripped from the slash on Rufus Greene's face. He wiped his hand across it, staring at it in disbelief, and then he looked back at the man, forgetting about me.

"What the fuck?" He moved away from him, and Johns moved closer, holding the knife firmly in his hand, ready to slash again.

"Go on," he said. "Go on."

"Do you want me to call the police?" I found my voice from somewhere, but I was barely able to speak. He didn't seem to hear me.

"I can't stand nothing hurting nobody lesser than they is. Can't stand nothing hurting something that's weaker than they is. Go on!!" He screamed the words out, as if he were shooing away some mangy, disgusting dog. Rufus Greene skulked down as if he were a wounded animal, holding up his bloody hands.

"Okay, man. I'm gone. I'm gone." His voice was a frightened whisper. Johns lunged toward his chest again with the knife, and Rufus moved back quickly, dodging as it slashed the air. He lunged forward again, the knife in his hands—a street fighter, sure of himself. Rufus turned and moved backward toward his car, not taking his eyes from his assailant. Johns followed him, stalking him, holding the knife down at his side like an avenging angel, and when he was satisfied that Rufus was gone, he turned toward me, saying nothing for a moment, a wildness in his eyes that frightened me. But then the rage and the residue of that violence disappeared, and when Johns spoke his voice was as accommodating as it had been when he'd brought me my car, thanked me for the tips.

"You okay?"

"Yes. I'm just lucky you came by. I don't know what I would have done if you hadn't." I was as out of breath as I would have been if I'd been fighting Rufus Greene. "Do you want me to call the police, give a report, tell them what has happened?" I asked again.

He seemed distracted, not looking at me when he answered "No." He glanced around nervously. "No police. I seen enough police." He looked back in the direction he had come from, muttering to himself as he turned, "I got to see somebody about something she been waiting for."

But he walked me to my car first, opened the door like a gentleman, and slammed it closed.

"Get along home now, lady," he said.

Still shaking from the experience, I did just that, thanking the powers that be that I was out of there and patting myself on the back for having given the man those five-dollar tips. And I was halfway home before I realized who it was he had come to see.

CHAPTER ELEVEN

HIS KNIFE WAS AT HER THROAT. HE HELD HER HANDS PINNED behind her back. If she moved an inch, he would cut her. Her eyes were closed, the lids fluttering slightly as if she were having some terrible dream. I hadn't noticed his face before, and I saw it now as if for the first time: the chin that seemed to have no bones; the strange muted color of the eyes stuck behind those cheap metal frames; the lips that sunk into themselves. He showed no expression, not even hatred, and he was dressed in black, like an executioner.

I had entered the house easily, cautiously opening the red oval door left ajar by Rufus Greene on his way to find and catch me. The house was quiet, deadly so, and my stomach grew tight at the thought of what might be there. I stole carefully through the silent rooms, knowing as I moved that this was how he'd done it—glancing cautiously up the twisting staircase, lingering for a moment in the spotless kitchen and small, neat dining room and finally pausing at the living room before I entered.

I didn't see them at first. The room was so quiet it could have been empty. Johns and Mandy stood away from the door, near the far wall. Taniqua sat on the pink and green sofa opposite them. An uncapped bottle of nail polish remover sat near a cardboard file on the mahogany table in front of her. Its acrid smell filled the room. Taniqua's eyes were as wide and frightened as those of a young doe, and she breathed uneasily, as if she couldn't quite catch her breath. She didn't look at her mother, but rather at Johns's face. He stared at Mandy Magic, whom he had pulled into his chest in a distorted reverse parody of a lover's embrace. The top of her head strained against his nose. One rough hand held the blade against her throat. The other held her arms. Although the room was cool, sweat formed and dripped down the small of my back. I could feel it under my arms and between my thighs.

He had surprised them. He must have found Mandy first, maybe in the kitchen fixing dinner or watching TV in her bedroom or coming down the staircase, thinking maybe of Kenton Daniels or Pauline Reese and the sorrow that had taken over her life. He had snatched her then, dragged her into the living room. What did she think when she saw him? Did she know then who he was and that he had come for her? Had he fooled her like he had everybody else?

He was a man who was easily forgotten; I could testify to that. He serviced the car, parked it, opened the door, closed it, accepted graciously any little tip that came his way without so much as a word or frown, never noticed, never getting in the way, like so many other old black men who park the cars and carry the groceries and sweep the floors. Part of the scenery. Like my father had been.

But this man was a killer, and he had been able to swoop into people's lives, disrupting nothing, then slaughter them swiftly with the knife he firmly held. He had easily placed those notes at her door, vandalized her car. He had gotten in and out of her building without being questioned or stopped. He had wrapped a phone cord around a woman's neck with his rough, powerful hands and squeezed it until the life came out of her because she had recognized him.

Something or somebody that had struck her as strange and that might be important, was what Pauline Reese had said to Karen. But she must have had no idea what this man was capable of doing to her. She had gone downstairs to the garage for some reason; maybe all that talk about her past had spurred her memory for faces. She'd seen him, recognized him, and let him know it. Maybe she'd even asked him what his name was and if he knew that Mandy worked there. She'd come back up, called me on the phone, and he'd come up behind her, opening and then slamming the door after he'd killed her. And Kenton Daniels had heard him.

So he had to kill Kenton Daniels too, because he didn't know what Kenton had heard or seen, and he couldn't take any chances. It was Kenton Daniels who brought Mandy Magic's fancy red car into the garage each morning. Kenton Daniels who paid him to wash the Lexus, gave him his tip, traded small talk about the Bulls or Lakers, talked about how lousy the weather had been. And with a sweep of guilt, I realized he had gotten Kenton Daniels's address from that notebook I had left on the hood of my car the night he killed Pauline, the one he had so thoughtfully left for me to find in my seat. He had gotten this address then too.

"Johns." I said his name. It felt strange saying it in this context, with my heart beating as fast as it was. I'd never meant to be condescending, but undoubtedly I had been in some small way during our occasional encounters. I was the lady with the money, doling out those five-dollar tips she couldn't afford. I'd been his "superior," listening to him being balled out by a boss fifteen years his junior. But he was the strong one now, the man with the plan and the power to kill, and he held his knife with an executioner's sense of duty. He glanced up at me; his hold on

Mandy Magic tightened. I could see the muscles in his hand grow taut. Awkwardly he shifted toward me, easing her with him. She opened her eyes then, staring straight ahead, seeing nothing. Her eyes had been robbed of everything, even fear. But when she shifted her gaze to Taniqua, something flashed in them—love, I realized, accompanied by such sadness it stunned me. She knew she was going to die. She was saying good-bye to the only person who mattered to her. I forced my eyes to leave her face, focusing instead on his.

"Johns."

"My name ain't Johns."

"What is it, then?"

He didn't say anything for a moment, and his eyes grew dim as if he had made some terrible decision.

Would he kill us all? What would it take for me to overpower him and take him by surprise? Maybe nobody would have to die. Too many had been killed by this man already. From somewhere inside, I pulled up the strength that always comes when I need it. I said a prayer to the folks that give it to me—my grandmother, my brother, my father, even my own mother who I knew had loved me despite everything she had done. I was sure of myself again. I was stronger than this man. I knew it in my soul. I tried to recall everything I knew about hostage negotiation, the moves to make and those to avoid. But I could think of nothing that would help us. It was going to come back to my God-given instincts, which it always did.

How could I connect with him?

"Johns," I said his name pleasantly this time, as if I were going to ask him out for a cup of coffee or a drink . He looked at me strangely.

"My name ain't Johns. I told you that. Tell her my name, Starmanda. Tell the lady my name." He snatched her toward him, arching her back, and she turned her face awkwardly and sharply to the side to avoid his blade.

"Tell her!"

"Odell."

"Louder!"

"I can't talk, Odell. I can't talk." There was an unmistakable note of familiarity in the way she spoke to him. She knew him from somewhere, knew him well. "Please let me go."

"Tell her my goddamn name!" He jerked her toward him again, straining her neck, flicking her chin with the tip of the knife, and then he loosened his grip on her, allowing her to talk.

"Odell Johnson." Her voice was clear and strong now, close to the voice the world knew. "His name is Odell Johnson." He pulled her to him again. Her eyes were open again but filled with terror, and I caught her gaze, my eyes asking her what I should say next, what he wanted from her.

"Tell her where you know me from."

"I don't—"

"Tell her where you know me from, goddamn you. Tell her where you know me from!"

"I grew up with him." There was utter defeat in her voice.

It was something in her past, their past. But how far back did they go?

I forced myself to look at his face and study his person. He seemed too old to have been her contemporary, but his looks were deceiving. They had fooled me. His ragged black clothes fit him too loosely. His cheap aviator glasses had struck me as out of place on his face the first time I saw him. I could see now that they had been broken and stuck together with a smudge of glue. His black sneakers were run-down and the laces were filthy; his black socks looked the same. From the first time I'd seen him, I'd sensed the despair that emanated from him; he had the smell of defeat. But he was spurred on by one purpose, and that alone had kept him focused—Mandy Magic.

Movin' on up.

I tried to remember the brief conversation we'd had the first time I saw him.

I ain't seen no diesels like this in a while. I been out of circulation.

He had spent time in prison; I was now sure of that. There were unmistakable signs: those institutional frames, the shuffle when he walked, the strength of his upper body. A person lost in time and mired in a past that others had left behind. What had he done? I wondered. How had Mandy been involved with him? Had they committed some crime for which only he had paid?

Odell Johnson. His first name and part of his last had been worn out on the shirt that he'd worn in the garage. Like the man himself, only a portion of him remained.

"Mr. Johnson," I said.

"Call me by my first name, Odell." It was an eerie reminder of the first time I'd met Mandy Magic, her insistence on being called Mandy. *Call me Mandy.*

"Odell." I geared myself up to gamble everything on the instincts my grandma gave me. "First of all, I'd like to thank you for keeping that man from hurting me. I didn't thank you outside, and I should have. Thank you for protecting me." I didn't give a damn about him or anything that he'd done for me, and I wondered if he could read through my lies, look into my heart as I tried to look into his. He seemed confused for a moment, as if he were trying to remember something that happened a while ago. A dull light came into his eyes.

"Okay."

"We have something in common," I ventured cautiously, watching Mandy again. She had opened her eyes again, and they shifted over to Taniqua on the couch, her thin young body doubled over as she sat, her hand over her mouth as if she were sick. But there was nothing I could do to help her. I made myself focus on Johnson.

"What? What do we have in common?" He looked puzzled. I

moved closer to him, just a very small step, wondering if I could get that knife without his using it. If I could distract his attention long enough for her to push him, then I could rush him. He was a strong, but slight man; with the two of us there might be a chance. I stared at Mandy's empty eyes, trying to get her attention, but there was nothing in them. No light. No understanding. It was as if she had given up all that she had.

What hold did this man have on her?

If I could understand that, I could understand his vulnerabilities, and I could disarm him.

"Well." I took another cautious step forward, casually and furtively, as if I were merely shifting my weight. "Well, what you said before about hurting little things—" He tightened his hold on her. I realized I'd made a mistake. I changed it quickly. "Weaker things. I believe that too." I smiled like a Girl Scout, shifted closer. Mandy closed her eyes again, shutting me out along with the rest of the world.

Keep them open, girl. Keep them open.

I prayed that she would read my thoughts. He stepped back, guessing I was up to something, and his hands held her closer as he leaned into her, speaking in her ear in a low voice that I could still hear.

"Been a long time ain't it, Starmanda?"

"Yes, Odell," she replied in a low, frightened voice. An obedient voice.

What hold did he have?

"You know them notes were from me?" He was speaking directly to her now, bending toward her, his arms still holding hers tight, the tip of the knife now at her throat. There was disdain mixed with pride in his voice. She nodded weakly, accepting it, taking it as her due.

"You knew I was coming for you sooner or later, that we was coming for you, didn't you? That we wasn't going to let you get away with it."

Who was "we"? Was there somebody else in the house?

My eyes shifted to either side, and I listened for any foreign sound, prepared for quick movement behind me. There was nothing.

"Yes, Odell."

"I got your money too. You know I got your money. I deserved that money, didn't I? For all you took from me, you phony bitch, for all you took from me." His voice was rough and had turned threatening. He pulled her toward him again, slamming her body against his again. He had been reminded of something, and he was suddenly in a rage about it. A low horrible gurgle came out of her throat. For one terrible moment I thought that he had done it, slid that knife below her chin. A sound, like a moan, came from Taniqua. I had forgotten about her. There was nothing I could do to comfort her. I turned again to Mandy Magic, wondering what thing she had taken from him.

"I didn't mean to hurt you, Odell."

"Everyday I said your name. I knew I'd make you pay. You knew it too, didn't you?"

"I didn't mean to hurt you, Odell. It wasn't my fault. You have to understand me."

"You told me. You promised me—"

"That was so long ago," she said, and her eyes were fully opened now. She strained to look at him from the corner of them, turning her head slightly. "We were kids then, Odell."

"You weren't a kid when it happened."

"Yes. I was. You know I was. And so were you." She spoke cautiously, as if she were actually explaining something to a child. There was a renewed look of determination in his eyes, though, and renewed strength rekindled from his anger. She had said the wrong thing. He pulled her toward him again.

What could I do or say, I wondered, to distract him. I threw something out, batting around in the dark like I had with Kenton Daniels yesterday. Bluffing him with knowledge I didn't have, as if I knew something more than I did, anything to keep him from making that one lethal stroke.

"Tyrone knew about it then?" I asked him. Maybe Tyrone had been the "we" or known about it at some point. But he had killed Tyrone as well. His eyes questioned me, not understanding what I meant.

"He thought he knew, but he didn't know shit. I knew that son of a bitch couldn't keep nothing to himself. He'd feel bad and tell her something sooner or later."

His face relaxed. The weak chin dropped. The hard line of his gums grew more visible in his jaw. I could hear Mandy's breath coming in short, fast gulps, as if she were trying to pull in more air than she could handle. He was sure of himself, and when I looked at the half-smile that had formed on his lips, I knew that he was enjoying this. And I knew that his enjoyment would give me some time.

If he was going to kill her, he would have done it when he'd first come in the door, upstairs if he had found her there or in the kitchen. He wouldn't have bothered to drag her into the living room. He liked her terror and the way she trembled against him. He had waited for and planned this moment for how long—five years, ten maybe? He was savoring it. He wanted something from her, an answer, an admission that only she could give him, but she hadn't yet given it.

If I were to save her life, I would have to figure out what that admission was, what he needed and why he wanted it. Odell Johnson was on a holy mission. He had killed three people to get to her, and killers who kill with that kind of planning and perseverance want more than blood. They want understanding—for a world that they have created in their own sick image. He had murdered with the arrogance of the truly evil, and he would want recognition of what he had done, for what it had taken for him to get to her and attain this goal. I could use that need against him, to gain myself some time.

But I would have to tread lightly and not alert or irritate him. So

I smiled coyly, admiringly, using the friendly voice I'd used when we first met, close to but not quite the seductive voice that Mandy Magic used each night to pull out secrets that nobody wanted to tell.

"So you thought that Tyrone Mason might tell her?"

"But he really didn't know shit."

"But he knew she had . . ." I hesitated for a moment, as I searched for the proper word, not wanting to poke some unknown fire that simmered within him, ". . . worked with Rufus Greene."

"Yeah. That was all he had on her. He thought he knew something, but he didn't know shit."

"And you knew him from before?"

"Tell her," he pulled Mandy again, hard against him. She stared at me, her eyes filled with a silent plea, and I knew I'd made a mistake. "Tell her, damn you. Where I know Tyrone Mason from?"

"Harold Mason." Her voice was apologetic. He loosened his grip, freeing his hold on her so that she could talk. "He knew Harold. Harold introduced us. Me and Odell. Harold introduced him to Tyrone."

So he had known Mandy through her cousin Harold. They must have met in high school. What had Pauline Reese said about her then? That she was wild and pretty and liked young, fast hoodlums, of which he had probably been one. Somewhere down the line, Harold Mason had introduced him to his son, Tyrone. Or maybe they had met at Harold Mason's funeral. Maybe their plan had been hatched that day.

" 'Me and Odell,'" he repeated Mandy, mockingly. " 'Me and Odell.' I used to hear your voice on that radio, Starmanda. Listening to you talking your shit like you know everything in the world, like you got your finger on God instead of the devil, and I thought about you and Odell. Me and you."

Was he some old high-school boyfriend, bitter about the way she'd left him, come to take his revenge for some imagined or real betrayal?

"If you knew Harold Mason so well, how could you kill his son?" I asked him, and he looked surprised for a moment, as if he hadn't quite thought things out. Taniqua uttered a muffled cry at the mention of Tyrone's name, and the sound of it startled me. I glanced at her again, sick because I could do nothing except play this thing out, knowing that the worst was probably yet to come.

"It was smart of you to kill him in the park. You're a smart man, Odell." I threw that out, disgusted by my words as I spoke them, but knowing it might put him at ease. His glance of appreciation made me felt bolder. If I could keep him talking, sooner or later I might find a way to stop him. He might weaken. We might stand a chance.

"And you knew Pauline too? You were in high school together?"

"I knew her. She wouldn't talk to me, though. Too good for me. Too good for her own good."

"And Kenton Daniels? You knew him too, and that was why you killed him?"

"I knew his father. *Doctor* Kenton Daniels, *Junior*. Right, Miss Starmanda Jackson. I knew his daddy, didn't I?" There was contempt and raw hatred in his voice.

"It wasn't what you thought," she said.

"It was everything I knew."

"I didn't do it—no matter what you say."

"And EB too. You think I didn't know about EB, and what you did and why you did it. I thought about it every day and night for what you did, the choice you made. Where you went when I was gone. What happened to Amanda."

The room grew still, as if old ghosts had been summoned and an invisible force had quietly entered.

"Amanda." I said the name aloud, hardly realizing I'd said it, letting it linger on my lips because it reminded me of the name I loved, and the way my grandmother would summon her sister's spirit. Starmanda. Amanda. He stared at me as if by saying the name I'd defiled it. But his eyes filled with tears, and his grip on Mandy Magic's shoulders loosened. The knife had dropped to his side now, as if that name had worked a gentle spell and taken away his rage, bringing in something else, another emotion.

"Amanda," he said the name back to me, and the rest of that first conversation we'd had that day came back as I recalled his eyes, how empty and haunted they had become and how filled with despair.

I had myself a real little daughter once too. A real teeny one, a long time ago. Every bit of light that shined in my life came and went with her.

"Amanda was your daughter, wasn't she?" It was a question I didn't need to ask because I knew by the quick look of apprehension that came to Mandy's face and the sigh that seemed to take everything out of Odell Johnson's body. That name was what had been between them—the old score that needed to be settled, the price that had to be paid. Mandy Magic stepped away from him, so slowly and cautiously she hardly seemed to move. He let her go, hardly noticing. She turned to face him. The knife hung still at his side, but he held it firmly. There was something else in his eyes, a deeper grief than I'd seen before. Mandy, too, seemed transfixed, as if she too had been transported to another time and place. Their eyes locked for a moment in some shared connection and then shifted apart.

"You killed her, didn't you?" His voice was barely a whisper.

Her trembling started with her lips and then worked itself down to her hands and fingers, and soon her body shook as if she were cold. The strength that she'd always been able to pull up was gone. She looked as small and fragile as she actually was, not even as big as her voice, which came out trembling through her hands, as if she were whispering some secret that should never be said aloud.

"She was sick, Odell."

"You killed her because of what that white man said he'd give you."

"No, Odell!" She backed away from him. He moved toward her.

"You killed her that night."

"No, Odell!"

"I left that morning. She was okay. Real little, but they said she would be all right. I come back late. Go to bed. Next day she's dead."

"You were drunk, Odell." It was an accusation mixed with anguish, and her statement made him step backward slightly, as if it was more than words—a destructive truth that I sensed he had never accepted. "Have you forgotten what happened that night?"

His eyes left hers, dropping in shame. She had the advantage now, and she used it against him. The old confidence was back, and with each word her voice grew firm and convincing, as steady as it was on the radio and as persuasive. Her words pelted him like stones.

"How old were you then, Odell, eighteen? Do you know how old I was? Seventeen, with a baby, your baby, and you just eighteen yourself, drinking, getting high so much that half the time you didn't know what day it was. And the baby was always sick—have you forgotten that?—how much she cried, how she wouldn't eat, how nothing we could do would please her."

"Call her by her name."

"And I was there by myself that night, Odell. You were drunk. And every night you came home with nothing on your mind but acid, booze, and sex, and the only thing I had going for me, the only way I'd made my own way till then, was when I was out there with Rufus. I was seventeen, for Christ's sake, Odell. Just out the house for two years, and I saw my whole life mapped out for me. Nothing. And . . ."

"Call her by her name."

"And you came in that night, fell out high. And she died during that night, when you were drunk. That's all. I went on with my life. You went on with yours. Can we let this go?" She said it like she was talking to a child, as if she knew what she was doing. She moved away from him, closer to the door, closer to me. "It was so long ago, Odell. That baby died so long ago. It's hard even for me to remember sometimes."

"Call her by her name. Amanda! Say her name!"

"And then when the doctor came that night, to that disgusting stinking little room not even fit for us to say nothing of a baby—don't you remember that room, Odell—and you said, it was better off that she was dead. Don't you remember, when the doctor came, and she was so little and feeble? Lying on the bed that night. You were drunk, Odell. Your mind played tricks on you like a drunk's will do."

She took a single step away from him, a baby step, like we used to call them when I was a kid. I could see what she was doing, how she would get away. Confusion was on his face as he tossed the facts around in his mind, the somber eyes narrowed behind the glasses, the tired mouth drawn in a line as he searched his memory for something to dispute what she was saying. I was sure for a moment that she had done it, that she had finally brought it back to him, that he was as guilty as she for whatever had happened to their child. I hoped that this nightmare would be over, that he would leave now. He had come and confronted Mandy Magic, and she had acknowledged what they both had shared. And now he knew his part in it and could leave her alone.

But then something came into his eyes, a flicker of emotion and feeling that told me she'd played it all wrong, and she'd pay the price for that now. He stiffened, calling her a liar with the tilt of his head, and the anger that came full force into his face, contorted it into a mask of rage. His voice was barely audible when he spoke but filled the room with its power. His words hitting her now, as hers had him.

"It took me damn near twenty years for it all to come back, what I saw that night. Ten years of getting drunk and pretending to forget it, living my life like it was full of nothing. Ten years in a place no man should be. Them nightmares robbing me of my rest, keeping me from my day. Making do with love and sex wherever I could get it, whatever I could get it from. All I could think of when I heard your voice on that damn radio was killing it, that *magical* voice you got. Swearing to myself I'd kill it, so I'd never have to hear it again or think of you again."

He stopped talking, not able to go on for a moment, and then he continued, as sure of himself as she had been a moment ago.

"Yeah, I was drunk that night. But I know what I saw."

"What did you see, Odell?" I asked the question this time, breaking into what they had started. *I* needed to know, and I couldn't leave it up to her anymore. But it wasn't between me and him, and it wasn't me he gave his answer to.

"She wouldn't stop crying that night. Her voice so loud and high like some whistle going off in your ear. And you picked her up that night, Starmanda, crying yourself. You brought her back to the bed with you, and I opened my eyes, Starmanda. Just for that moment, while you shook her hard, Starmanda, like she was some rag doll made of cloth. That little white dress I bought her waving like a dirty flag, her neck whipping back like she wasn't even human. You shook her and shook her, until there wasn't nothing left of her to shake. I saw you do that, Starmanda, and there wasn't nothing I could do about it but lay there and watch you. Just lay there like a dog and watch."

"I had to make her stop crying," Mandy said, as if she were telling him something that she'd just learned herself.

"Be quiet. Don't say anything else," I told her then, whispering, not sure even that she heard me, but knowing that she was making a mistake by going on with it. I knew the truth she had to tell should stay unsaid. I knew now that it could never be enough for him, and that her truth, whatever it was, would never be his. Yet I also knew she had to tell it. That there was something within her that needed to get straight, and by telling it she would finally accept what she had done. And so she told it, stepping forward, facing him, owning up to it in his face.

"But she was going to die anyway." Her eyes pleaded with him. "I knew that. Dr. Daniels had told me as much, warning me, trying to prepare me, although he knew well enough that I'd welcome it. I prayed for it."

He drew back from her, as if she'd slapped his face, putting his hands over his ears, trying to keep her words out, but the way his face broke, then came together and broke again as she went on told me that he heard every word.

"He knew I had shaken her before, that something was wrong, and if you hadn't been so drunk, you would have known it too, but you were the big man, even though you weren't nothing but a kid yourself, as scared as me."

"I could have made things work for us, Starmanda. If you'd let me—"

"You couldn't give her shit because you didn't have shit. So when she would cry—again and again—through the night, through the day, and there was nobody to turn to, all I had was me—I'd shake her until she stopped, and that night . . ." She paused slightly, crying to herself now as she talked, her words muffled and hard to understand. "And when she started, I shook her and shook her, like Mrs. Mason used to shake me, and she went to sleep, and then when you came home, drunk again, high again, and she cried some more, and I shook her and shook her and shook her until she stopped."

It was as if the breath had been taken from us all in that room when she said it, and then she continued, speaking evenly, her voice matter of fact.

"I called Dr. Daniels then. He was a good man. I was six months gone by the time I got to him with that baby I didn't want, and he wanted me to give her up, but I knew you would never stand for that and I wasn't strong enough, with my belly hanging over my pants. I didn't want to go back to Rufus, and I thought you might be a way out.

"And he didn't tell all he knew that night because he was a decent man and he knew that her death had set me free. He had seen that longing in my eyes when I looked at that picture of Kenton sitting all neat and happy in his mama's pretty garden, and I told him once, 'I'm going to have me a baby like that, one day, sitting in a garden like that,' and he told me I could do anything in this world I wanted to if I put my mind to it. And I decided right then I'd put my mind to it."

I glanced at Taniqua. She had been a silent witness to this as I had. She sat stone-like on the couch, her dark eyes seeing everything, yet understanding little. My eyes shifted back to Odell and the knife that was now hitting his thigh in a hard, irregular rhythm. He stood an arm's length away from her. He moved forward. She did not step back.

"Can you forgive me, Odell?" She begged him, but his eyes were hard, and there was no forgiving anywhere to be seen in them. He moved toward her again, and I knew then what would happen, that he hadn't gotten what he'd come for, and I could feel the hair move on the back of my neck. She must have sensed it, too, as she backed away from him now, a step, maybe two, nearer to me but not close enough. He moved with her in some strange mock dance, his hand still on that knife, the rhythm of it hitting his loose black jeans, stronger now, more emphatic.

"You have to forgive me," she said, but Mandy Magic was not used to begging and her voice gave her away. It was too much like the one we all heard at night, too convincing, too seductive, and I knew that she had risen up too high, and he had slipped too low, for her to really want his forgiveness. He knew it too. She spoke reasonably then, like you might to somebody who was calm and reasonable even though he wasn't either. I couldn't understand why she couldn't see that, why she wouldn't drop it. "Can't you understand that after all these years, Odell? Can't you understand that I saw the light at the end of the tunnel for me, and I had to move toward it?"

"But *she* was my light. Amanda was *my* light and you shook my light out."

He moved as quickly as he had moved toward Rufus Greene, as quickly as he must have moved toward Kenton Davis and Tyrone Mason, with a slash so swift I barely saw it until her blood dripped in a thin red line across the middle of her throat. She gazed at him in disbelief and then crumpled to her knees before him, clutching her throat as if she were begging him for her life, and I heard somebody scream. I thought it was Mandy for a split second. But then I knew.

"Mama!" she cried out. "Mama! Mama! Don't let him hit you again!" Each word went through me as painfully if they had been my own.

The fancy pistol from the mahogany case was in Taniqua's hand before I knew she'd gone for it. One shot brought him to his knees, and then she stood over him as if she were in a dream and emptied the gun into him until he was dead, killing him as she had killed another man before he could hit her mother again.

I don't know how much time passed before I got myself together enough to call an ambulance and finally the police. Maybe it was ten minutes, maybe fifteen. It hadn't made too much of difference one way or the other, they told me later. I do know that moments after it happened, I held Taniqua in my arms as she trembled, holding on to me for dear life—through the bustle and questions of the medical technicians as they worked in hushed silence to save her mother's life, through the thoughtful, probing questions of the police, through the kindness of the social worker and the distance of the hospital staff as we waited to find out if Mandy Magic would live.

And as we waited, I thought about what had happened over the last two weeks, and small things, seemingly unimportant when I first encountered them, began to take on a clearer meaning and make some sense. I remembered the photograph that Taniqua had shown me and the despair and resignation on the young Starmanda Jackson's face. She had been holding her own child that day, and Odell had probably been the proud young papa, holding the camera to take a picture of his firstborn, her mother and his friend, Harold Mason. The angels in her life, those two men she mentioned so often, had had their "devilish" sides. Elmer Brewster had been a lecherous John whose tastes had run to sixteen-year-old prostitutes. Dr. Kenton Daniels, Jr., had been a physician who looked the other way when she murdered her child.

And she had kept it all inside, the contradictions, lies, and private anguish. Had she worn all that red to tie her to a past she was afraid to claim? I wondered. It was the color suggested by the pimp who had stomped nearly to death the man who had first abused her. She had also kept "Mandy" for Starmanda, never giving up the whole of her, keeping what she could of that long-gone part of herself. She had tried to live her life honorably—helping those in need, reaching out as much as she could, saving a girl whose life had been as troubled as her own. But in the end her past had stalked her, movin' on up to claim what belonged to it.

Yet Mandy Magic's luck held. Her long-dead mama was still looking out. Odell Johnson didn't kill her. His knife slashed through her larynx and trachea but missed by an inch her carotid arteries, so she survived his attack. But she would never again speak above a whisper. So, in the end, he did what he had sworn he would do. He stole her light, as she had stolen his.

EPILOGUE

NOBODY LIKES TO THROW MUD ON A WOMAN WHO TRIUMPHS over tragedy, so the story Mandy Magic told the world was quickly accepted as the whole truth. She said she had been stalked by a madman named Odell Johnson, who murdered her two best friends, injured her throat, and was killed in self-defense by her daughter. My name and presence were left out of it completely. The story was front-page news for a couple of days and slipped out of the papers altogether by the end of the week.

After she got out of the hospital, I phoned to see how she was doing, but she never returned my calls. I even drove by her house one night, but she'd put it up for sale shortly after the incident. A spokesperson later announced that she was retiring from her radio show to devote herself to raising her daughter and running her stations. She became as impossible to touch as she'd been before I met her. She did, however, send the money she owed me, and I was glad to get it. I knew I'd never hear from her again. Keeping secrets is a hard habit to break.

In the days that followed, I found myself more depressed than I wanted to admit. Things still seemed unsettled, and I felt like I'd been left holding a bag filled with somebody else's emotional garbage. I had been involved with her less than two weeks, but everything about her case took a toll on my spirit. I handled my depression the way they warn you not to. I told my kid I had the flu, crawled into bed with a bag of Famous Amos chocolate chip cookies, and did nothing but sleep and watch soaps and late-night movies all day and most of the night. It was in this sorry state that Jake Richards found me.

He dropped by early one morning with a quart of orange juice and some blueberry muffins and knocked cautiously on my bedroom door.

"Jamal let me in. If you want me to leave, just say so," he said. I knew the moment I heard his voice that there was nobody else I wanted to see. Besides my son, he was the only man alive I would let see me in this condition.

"I heard a rumor about an unidentified woman in that scene at Mandy Magic's and figured it might be you," he said as he settled down on the foot of my bed. He leaned over and touched my forehead gently with the palm of his hand. "No fever. When do you plan to get up?"

"I don't."

"Maybe you should tell me what *really* happened that night," he said, and I poured it all out in a torrent of curses and tears. When I finished, he shook his head sadly and hugged me.

"It all started when she killed her baby."

"It all started when he couldn't forgive her for doing it," Jake corrected. "But she never really forgave herself."

"She shook Amanda to death. That's called Shaken Baby Syndrome, and that's considered murder."

"And there's never a moral excuse for it, but historically speaking, neonaticide is not as rare as you might think, particularly before *Roe v. Wade*. There are even textbook theories that in certain cases and in some societies, it's biologically wired, and that a girl who is as poor and desperate as Mandy Magic was will sacrifice her unhealthy offspring to ensure her own survival and that of her future children."

"And you believe that?"

He shrugged noncommittally. "Textbook theory."

"I just can't get over the fact that every time I looked at that man I thought about my father."

Jake gave me a half-smile. "There's a little bit of Odell Johnson in the best of us," he said after a moment. "There's always that part of you that wants to get even, that won't allow somebody the grace of redemption. Life is more complicated than black and white or right and wrong, so you've got to give yourself permission to understand the gray, to let the sun sneak in whenever it can."

"But there does seem to be a lot of gray," I said skeptically, and he dropped his eyes.

"There always is."

We sat there for a while, not saying much else, laughing a little, munching the muffins, sharing the juice until I felt better, and it was time for him to go to work. And I realized after he left just how much he meant to me and how much I'd missed him. I didn't know what would become of our relationship, how far it would go, what would be the final word or deed that would bind us together or tear us apart. I just knew that too many shadows had fallen into our lives for me to throw this piece of sunshine away.